CW00411134

Grumpy
Old Git

Surviving In A World You No Longer Understand

James Hulme
Grumpy Edition

Grumpy Old Git

I am suffering from the most horrendous case of man flu ever experienced by human kind. If you are a man you will know what this is like and you will recognise the complete lack of sympathy and empathy shown by the female of the species towards this awful affliction.

As my nose drips onto my keyboard and my head pounds with each press of the keys, I realise that this may not be the best condition to be in when writing this book. However, if my head was clear I might be in danger of falling into the trap of clemency and give undue leniency to the problems I am about to discuss with you.

Before I get into this any further I feel a warning is appropriate. I wasn't always grumpy. My grumpiness crept up on me slowly and then unexpectedly pounced when I wasn't looking. Had I seen it coming, or been aware of it I could have stopped it, but I didn't. Many of the things I am about to talk about will be familiar to you. You probably won't have thought much about them before, but once you become aware of them it cannot be undone. Much like walking in on your geriatric grandmother on the toilet, these things can't be unseen.

With that unsettling image planted firmly in your head, let's replace it with another. If you have been bought this book by a friend, family member or significant other, then it is very likely they see you as being on the wrong end of the grumpy spectrum. You may not have realised that they see you this way, you may even think you are the least grumpiest person you know. Don't distress though, take this as a green light to up your grumpy game. Embrace it, nurture it. True grumpiness takes time, effort and dedication. Don't bottle it now.

Just like earthquakes, grumpiness has a scale. From the mild mannered frustration invoked by Frank Spencer in Some Mothers Do 'Ave 'Em, to the top of the scale where good old Victor Meldrew reigns supreme (I don't believe it!) Good old Victor is the epitome of grumpiness and what we should all aspire to reach. Like Victor, you are probably driven to grumpiness by the people around you and the unbearable and unrelenting stupidity of modern life. That is the root cause of your distress. Do not despair, you are not alone. There is an ever growing band of men, brothers of bewilderment if you will, that are finding these modern times utterly frustrating and debilitatingly tedious. I hope you find solace in the passages that follow and can take comfort in the fact that we are the sane ones. We are the last bastion of logic in a world that has gone completely sideways.

Without further ado lets kick off with the first item of business, 5 tell tail signs that you may be grumpy. Or as I prefer to call them the 5 commandments which, unlike the more established biblical rules, should be easier to live by as there are only half as many.

Note: Some names, dates and places have been changed in order to protect the stupid, the dull and the inept, however some have not.

5 Signs You May Be Grumpy

1. You find that going out of the house, for whatever reason is now just not worth the hassle. You find good reasons not to go to anywhere. Restaurants serve unpleasant food, it's too loud to have a conversation and it is too expensive. You use the same excuse when it comes to the cinema, the pub, the theatre or your wife's friends house. The last one also comes with the added excuse of "what again? We saw them last Christmas!" Additional excuses include the traffic is too heavy, pedestrians get in the way or it's simply just raining...again.

2. You have started to notice people, particularly the young, are using a strange unknown dialect. You can detect the odd word of English but it's becoming less and less common. You hear things like "Bae, Bff, LOL, 5G, the cloud, Siri and bling but you have no idea what they mean, and who is this Alexa person? She seems popular. You seem to be getting left behind, technology is changing faster and faster. You have only just mastered

your mobile phone but even that is 10 years out of date, apparently, and what the hell is smart TV? From what I see TV is dumber than ever.

3. You find you have a strange sense of "I just don't care". This covers all aspects of life. You no longer care about offending someone, in fact you are beginning to go out of your way to offend people. You have no interest in clothes or fashion. "Whats wrong with what you have?" you ask. It works, it is in one piece and it covers all the important droopy bits. When this ceases to be the case, you will replace it with a similar and equally functional item.

4. Perhaps you have found conversations have become somewhat strained. You used to be able to engage in a meaningful and constructive exchange of ideas but now all your conversations seem to be complaint orientated, usually about health, money, the weather, the young or how things just aren't what they used to be. On the rare occasion when a conversation appears to be normal it won't take long to transform into some sort of

crusading rant, even if it was only your wife asking if you wanted a coffee.

5. At one time you were filled with love and compassion for the world. You were concerned about endangered species, the plight of global warming and in extreme cases even unemployment figures and inflation rates. You may have been a child of the 60s with the ideals to match but lately this has changed. Now you find the phrases "serves them right," "not my problem" or "tough luck" rolling off the tongue. Often interspersed with a range of toe curling expletives that would embarrass Bernard Manning. These outbursts may come as a surprise to those around you, but remember you don't care about offending people anymore.

If you can relate to any of this then there is the real possibility that you are in fact seen by others as grumpy. This should be embraced, nurtured and developed. So let's begin.

Petrol Hell

Unfortunately with life being totally dependant on petrol and diesel these days it is inevitable that you will frequent one of these horrible places on an almost daily basis. I have been in quite a few over my lifetime and I am convinced they are the personification of hell itself, or at the very least some form of purgatory.

Petrol stations used to be great places. I used to love going there with my dad when I was a kid to fill up the car with Four Star. You could even collect tokens and after a year or two of fastidious collection, exchange them for a nice set of wine glasses or a torch or something else that would be discarded in the back of the cupboard a week later.

In those simpler days petrol stations sold petrol, maybe bread and milk and the occasional Mars bar or box of Ferrero Rocher if you lived in a posh town. All this stuff was sold alongside a forest of Magic Tree air fresheners and a sea of two stroke engine oil. The lights were dim, the floor was stained and the door usually squeaked loudly when opened. The more astute amongst you will probably realise where i'm heading with this.

The once quaint purveyor of petrol has slowly overtime morphed into what can only be described as a mini supermarket. Some even house post offices and delicatessens, who as a sideline occasionally sell petrol. The idea of just going there to buy petrol is absurd. You may think this is a good thing. Convenient you might even say, but don't be fooled. Let me walk you through it.

It's 8am and you're on your way to work, but because you were too tired to stop on the way home last night, you are reminded with an annoyingly loud bong that you need petrol. So you pull into your local petrol station with the simple and mundane thought of purchasing a few litres of the magical go-go juice. Now the irritation begins. You pull up to a pump, open the fuel cap and insert the nozzle of your chosen fuel and wait. Then you wait, and wait and wait and then wait some more. It seems to take a lifetime for the cashier to press a button and activate your pump. With each passing second the anger builds and with each tick of the clock you're left standing there, nozzle in hand, looking like the guy who stands at a urinal for longer than is socially acceptable when his plumbing has malfunctioned. You avoid all eye contact and impatiently pull the pump in a vain attempt that something will come out.

You may think this is the cashiers fault. This may well be true if they don't like you. However it is more likely that they are up to their necks in someones weekly shop or have popped over to the deli counter to weigh out a few portions of artisan ham for one of the school mums. Incidentally it is likely her 4x4 that's blocking one of the fuel pumps and they likely weren't buying fuel anyway.

Eventually you get the fuel into your car and replace the fuel cap but, due to your haste and much like a rushed visit to the little boys room, some fuel will have dribbled down the side of the car and will require wiping. Leaving your hands and anything else you touch smelling of petrol for the next 300 years.

Then comes the nightmare of actually paying for the stuff. You take a deep breathe and run the gauntlet towards the tills. You skilfully sidestep the chatting busybodies who have nothing to do and nowhere to be except in your way. You spot several people with baskets overflowing with cauliflower, chips and cat food and you know they are heading for the till. You must beat them to it if you stand any chance of getting out of there anytime soon. You zigzag your way through the aisles and just as the end is in sight, tragedy strikes. You join the back of the slowest moving queue in all of human history. You will know the people ahead of you, they are the same in every petrol station. There is old Edna with 27 vouchers for her cat food and insists she's got the right change in her purse, but she is blind as a bat and asks the cashier to identify each coin she extracts from her cobwebbed purse. Then we have Deirdre with her 3 screaming kids. She has brought her basket of goods to the till but unfortunately after ringing half of them through she realises she's forgotten half of what she went in for. She scurries off down the aisles to retrieve the rest of her shopping, leaving behind her terrible kids to torture the cashier, mess with the displays and have a mini riot.

Then there is old John. He's a kind old man who likes to talk to everyone. He thinks he is being friendly and polite. What he's really doing is holding everything up until he collects his pension, danders home, sits in a chair, reads his paper and inevitably falls asleep after the first dozen words.

Meanwhile as more people join the queue, the cashier starts to sweat. They begin to frantically hit the big red button calling for all available operators to attend the tills, but no one comes. They are much too busy stacking the shelves and putting up posters about the deals of the week. Eventually the tills clear and you reach the purveyor of petrol. Don't get excited it's not over, not by a long chalk.

You efficiently state "pump number 3, £20 of unleaded" This should be all the cashier needs to complete your transaction, but they have other ideas. "Is that everything sir?" "Yes," you reply hoping this will be an end of it. It's not. Next they try to flog you a packet of biscuits or buns or some such rubbish. "Can I interest you in a packet of Jaffa Cakes? It's the deal of the week, only 50p." You politely say "no" while in your head you're thinking, "If I wanted bloody Jaffa Cakes I would have lifted a packet before now, just let me pay for my bloody petrol."

Eventually you are allowed to hand over the cash but then the big one comes. "Do you have a nectar card sir?" At this stage even if you have one you just say "no" in some sort of vain last ditch attempt to escape. However they still have you in their clutches. They will try and engage you in conversation. "Nice weather" they'll say expecting to kick off some form of meaningful interaction. Now what you should really say is "It was nice until I came in here, now its awful. I have a headache from those screaming kids, I'm late for work and to top it all off you want to start the same inane conversation with me that you had with all six of the people in front of me, will you bollocks. Take your Jaffa Cakes and shove them up your artisan ham slicer". Instead what comes out is something like "yes it is warm for this time of year" or some such piffle. You have bottled your first chance of the day to let your grumpiness flow out.

Angry and under pressure you trudge back to your car, get in, start the engine and try to move forward but you can't. You're surrounded on all fronts by abandoned cars and delivery vans.

Are you feeling irritated yet? I am just by writing it. You wait, eyeballing everyone coming out the door, trying to match each person to their respective car, hoping they will get into the one in front of you thus allowing you to make a clear dash to freedom from the petrol prison. Eventually the carefree owner saunters back to their vehicle. All is well and you are free to continue your journey unencumbered. That is once the person in front has sorted out their handbag, checked their makeup, sent a text message or two or whatever else it is people spend their time doing at this point. By now you have slumped forward, head on the steering wheel and cursing all of civilisation.

Now you may say that in this day and age I should embrace modern technology and use things like "Pay At the pump". This certainly would negate the need to deal with people and go some way to ease the stress and tedium suffered in filling up. However I would urge caution with this approach. I treat these machines much in the same way I treat ATM machines. I rarely use ATM machines partly because they are usually covered in vomit, spit or other bodily fluids of an unknown origin, but mostly because putting your card into one of these machines means there is a fair chance an unscrupulous Romanian will help himself to the contents of your bank account. The stress suffered from trying to retrieve your hard earned cash from Eastern Europe is second only to that suffered during the aforementioned petrol station visit.   Is that a risk you want to take?

All this just to put a few gallons of petrol in the car so you can travel to a place you really don't want to go to, just so you can earn a wage, most of which will likely be spent on petrol from a place you really don't want to go to.   The only slight glimmer of hope is that you don't actually work in a petrol station. If you do then I owe you no sympathy.

Fear and Loathing In The Nanny State

The cotton wool attitude of people these days really irritates me, but before I dive head first into the quagmire that is health and safety let me just say that I do agree with some aspects of it. Wet floor signs for example are a good idea. They can save you from a nasty injury or at least the embarrassment of falling head over arse in public. Providing the floor washer hasn't put the sign in a such a stupid place that the only way you will see it is when you ironically trip over it. Mind your head signs are also useful to those of us blessed with height and I'm sure all the procedures and safety measures put in place over the years to aid the disabled or impaired are an excellent idea and highly beneficial to those that need them.

I have no problem whatsoever with any of these but what irritates me more than anything is the constant barrage of unnecessary and blatantly stupid warnings and advice that so called health and safety officials and political correctness crusaders have bestowed upon us. These people must be the most boring plonkers on Gods green earth.   Everything must be risk assessed and checked for the slightest iota of offensiveness or danger incase we drown in the tears of the stupid and the over sensitive.

The legendary Scottish comedian Billy Connolly once told a story about a strange warning he found on a hairdryer in a hotel room that he happened to be staying in. I assumed that this was an exaggerated story made up for comic effect. How foolish I was to doubt the great Sir William. During a recent overnight stay at a well known chain of hotels, the hairdryer in the room had emblazoned across it the warning "DO NOT USE IN THE SHOWER".   I read this several times to make sure I wasn't hallucinating or suffering from some form of undiagnosed dyslexia.   I had the same reaction as Billy and considered calling the reception desk to ask exactly who this warning was meant for. I can only conclude that they must have suffered from a spate of guests accidentally electrocuting themselves drying their hair while still in the process of actually washing it. Perhaps its aim was to provide a clue to the distressed and over worked travelling salesman who can't find a toaster to throw in the bath. A sort of wink wink nudge nudge, this will work too kinda thing.

Im sorry but I have to side with Billy on this one, if you are stupid enough to use an electrical device in the shower then you deserve to be culled from the herd.

It doesn't stop there. Other examples include coffee cups warning that the contents may be hot. I'd bloody hope so, who wants cold coffee? I'm not a Millennial guzzling down iced lattes. Hot water taps with an ugly warning label stating caution hot water. Again, I'd like to think so. Like most of you I am a reasonably intelligent and observant person and if I want hot water I will seek out the hot tap and be capable of assessing the temperature of the water before I stick my face into it.

Did you know plastic bags pose a danger of suffocation or that jigsaws contain small parts? I bought a pair of scissors with a warning on the packet telling me that the product would be sharp and to exercise extreme caution when using. I know the world has been dumbing down lately but my God has it really got this bad?

Being the modern gentleman that you are, you will have no doubt undertaken the task of laundry. Not voluntarily of course, but out of necessity. At some stage you will have reached into the drawer only to discover that the supply of clean pants has been depleted. You could just buy new ones or go commando but thats not very debonaire and after all we are not French. Laundry must be done and you will likely use one of those liquid tab things that are popular these days. Did you have the urge to eat one of them? No? But the packet clearly states "DO NOT EAT". This means that at some point someone has. Again like the hairdryer and hot water thing this should be common sense. If you need to be told this then see previous comment reference culling. This includes all those people who took part in the recent fad of filming themselves eating these pod things and posting it on the FaceTube for other similarly minded dimwits to copy. The world can do without this stupidity.

Health and safety permeates almost every aspect of our daily lives these days but there is one place that I can guarantee will have gone over the top with the whole thing. Government and official buildings. I think of these places as the epicentre of madness and bureaucracy. All day everyday men in boring suits with plain faces, dull cars and sensible shoes seep out of these buildings like an oil slick. Armed with a clipboard and bereft of humour they roam across the land risk assessing anything that comes in their way.

Even the weather cannot escape the clutches of these hard hat hi-visibility enthusiasts. Years ago Michael Fish would have come on the TV and said, "It is going to be windy with a spot of rain" and with the exception of a missed hurricane in 1987, that would be the end of it. Now a patch of persistent drizzle requires a weather warning of some sort. What would have been a windy day twenty years ago now comes with a stern warning to stay indoors or you will surely be killed. A light frost and the country comes to a standstill, some light rain and it floods and a spot of mild sunshine causes a drought. This irritates me. Why can we not cope with weather. It's one of the most commonly talked about topics in this country. I bet you can't go one day without someone talking about the weather. I've mentioned it at least twice so far.

Apart from unnecessary weather warnings, the one warning on TV that really gets my goat is the one that tells you "The following programme contains strong language, violence and scenes of a sexual nature." Who would have thought that,"Zombie Strippers From Hell" or "Theres An Axe Wielding Murderer Living In The Attic" were not children's TV programmes. I mean what are you expecting from a title like that, Songs of Praise perhaps, the Antiques Roadshow or blood curdling hatchet murder?

One that really irritated me lately was an announcement before an old episode of Porridge with the late great Ronnie Barker. A concerned mans voice emanated from the TV at the start of the programme alerting me to the fact that "the following programme contains outdated Language". This irritates me beyond believe, but my irritation soon turned to disbelieve when it became apparent that any scene that was deemed to be culturally insensitive or a bit close to the line was simply cut out altogether. This left huge chunks of the show missing. Apart from ruining a classic TV show, why have a warning alerting people that they may be offended when anything deemed mildly offensive was going to be cut out anyway? I felt cheated.

People seem to think it is their inalienable right to be offended, even by pure simple facts. If I was to say that crime is generally more prevalent in poorer areas of the country some well meaning social equality warrior would want a word with me. They would probably tell me that I could not say this and drone on about how it offends the poor and that really capitalism or an entrenched social hierarchy is to blame for all the crime. They would have you believe that the local gang of miscreants graffitied the local bus stop last night because Lord Sugar drives a Bentley and because Elton John doesn't get his glasses on the national health.

A good example of the need to be offended these days is evident in the channel 4 series of programmes titled, "It Was Alright In The….70s, 80s, 90s etc". This programme showed clips of shows from each of the previous decades that by todays standards simply would not be allowed to be made never mind shown on TV. Then, well-meaning personalities comment on these clips and without fail they all looked shocked, insulted and appalled by what they had just seen. However you can tell that inside they are bursting with laughter, but they must maintain a stern face and tut in disgust as that conforms to the social norms of today. They forget however that at the time of their making the world was a very different place. This doesn't make it right to say or do these things today but surely these things should be viewed in the context of their time. They simply can't be viewed through todays eyes and they certainly should not be censored out of history. It would be much more beneficial to use these inappropriate clips to show how far the world has moved on in the past 50 years. Don't be offended, instead appreciate where we are and where we have come from, and if you find it funny laugh anyway, as long as the man with the clipboard and brightly coloured vest isn't around to wag his finger at you.

I think people have lost the ability to think for themselves and make their own decisions. We have to be constantly told do this, don't do that and watch out for this. The problem is that although it's irritating I fear that if the nanny state disappeared overnight so too would large swaths of the population. Then again is that necessarily a bad thing?

Let's take a case in point. The once rough and ready enterprise of the handy man is one profession that has been hit squarely in the face with the cotton wool cannon. I recently bought a new cooker. My old one had served me well but its time had come to pass and my pies were coming out as cold as when they went in. The new cooker was delivered promptly along with the promise of installation and the removal of the now defunct appliance. It was all part of the service they said. The reality was somewhat different.

At exactly 0900hrs the doorbell rang. That should have roused my suspicions, a delivery arriving at exactly the arranged time? I should have known better. I opened the door and was greeted by a burly man with heavy boots and a beard to match. He certainly looked like he knew what he was about. "Cooker for you" he said and he began to wheel in the new appliance. He proudly placed the cooker in the centre of my kitchen floor and said, "There ya go sir, if you could sign here i'll be on my way." As I pushed the docket back in his direction without a signature, a look of puzzlement and bewilderment befell his face. I explained that he was to remove the old appliance and install the new one, as agreed at the time of purchase. "Oh no" he exclaimed, "Im just dropping off, Im not qualified to touch anything like that". I showed him my receipt and he scurried off to his lorry to make a series of phone calls to whoever was in charge of decision making, probably a health and safety person. He returned sometime later and concluded that I was in fact right. He explained how confused he was that they had sent him to do this job because apparently I needed a specialist. After consulting with his superior it became apparent that such a specialist would not be available for at least a week and it was arranged that I would get a £85 discount for the inconvenience. However, they refused to remove the old cooker even if I disconnected it. Presumably incase I somehow plunged the screwdriver into my chest cavity and they became implicated in some sort of culinary Cluedo murder bid. The delivery driver did it in the kitchen with the screwdriver sort of thing.

Long story short, I dismissed the bearded delivery driver, turned off the power, disconnected the three wires powering the old cooker and wired them into the new one. Job done. No one died, no one lost any limbs, no one got sued and it was all done in the absence of a hard hat or high visibility vest.

As the resourceful and attentive husband that I am, I thought this would be the perfect opportunity to get the wife something she had wanted for years. She always said she would love a kitchen with a stylish island in the middle, but apparently an old cooker with a sheet over it wasn't what she had in mind. Anyone know a man with a van and a high-vis vest?

The World Has Woke But I'm Still Sleeping

The After Eight dinner mint has been around since the early 60s. These little chocolate delights arrived on the table 20 years before the Ferrero Rocher started to roll of the production lines. While the little hazelnut ball was the preserve of ambassadorial get togethers, the After Eight was to be found at every single dinner party since the middle class fondue enthusiasts of Britain first decided to socialise together. While the Rocher was delicious, the golden blanket covering it and the popular pyramid formation always made this sweet seem rather too showy even bordering on gauche. The mint was much more regal. Housed in a dark green box, each one lined up in individual silk like pouches, they were presented to the table with a subtle cough and a gloved hand by the ever discrete Jeeves.

Apparently they are still churning out a billion of these little squares each year, but when was the last time you had one? I'm betting it was probably around 1998. Strangely this was around the time when the dinner party died out.

Think about it, apart from the contestants on "Come Dine With Me" who only do it because of the lure of cash, when did you last have what you would call a dinner party? Sure you might have had another couple round for a bite to eat but in general people tend to just meet at a restaurant instead. Why? The answer came to me a few weeks ago when another couple invited themselves round for dinner.

It was a Friday morning and an excited friend named Colin called me just as I was finishing breakfast. In order to protect his identity and his relationship I will call him Frank. Frank said he was keen for us to meet his new girlfriend Jessica. It was decided that they would come round that evening and I would cook a meal for them. Frank said that he had to warn me that Jessica was a pescatarian. I said I didn't care what her religion was, all are welcome here, even a Methodist. Frank corrected me and informed me that it wasn't a religion and that it meant Jessica didn't eat meat. Steak was off the menu but fish and vegetables were apparently fine.

At 7pm the door bell rang, Frank and Jessica had arrived. After the introductions and coats had been hung up I offered drinks. Frank opted for wine while Jessica said she would wisely avoid alcohol because she was driving. No problem but I became suspicious when the offer of a soft drink was also turned down. She explained this was because Coca Cola was a multinational conglomerate and she viewed it as exploitative and evil and it had no place in a right thinking modern home. Water was deemed acceptable provided it didn't come from a tap because the council had apparently been adding fluoride to it and that was bad. I went to the fridge to see if anything in there would be acceptable. As I rummaged through the contents of the cold cupboard I became aware that to Jessica my fridge probably would have looked like a scene from the Texas Chainsaw Massacre. There were various pieces of cow, some sliced up pigs and parts of a shaved sheep and I wasn't entirely sure how she would react to the carton of chilled cow juice either. Having located a bottle of flavoured water I decided to close the fridge door and not open it again for the rest of the evening incase it induced some form of meat based freakout.

Small talk was commenced but it didn't flow easily. Jessica liked her cows to aimlessly lie in a flowery meadow all day beside a babbling brook, while I liked my cow medium-rare and lying on a plate beside some pepper sauce. It was apparent that Jessica had some very different views to me. This was fine. That's the great thing about being human, everyone is different. Free to express themselves and live their lives in any way they see fit. I have no problem with how you live and I enjoy hearing and understanding other people's point of view. This is how we learn new things and develop into well rounded people. Jessica did not seem to be this way inclined. She seemed determined to convert me. It became apparent that she did not view this as a simple meal with new friends but rather some form of crusading intervention to save me from my destructive and ignorant ways.

Dinner was served. A full review of the plate was carried out. The news wasn't good. The vegetables were wrong because they were probably not organic. The smoked cod was probably wrong too because it was likely caught in a net and not on an environmentally conscious linc. This was becoming tedious. I'll spare you all the details of the rest of the meal but suffice to say all aspects of it were wrong. I might as well have clubbed a baby seal to death right there on the table and served it with a side of snow leopard. The coffee was wrong because it wasn't ethically sourced and came from a region of South America that was very bad. I thought the Columbian coffee business actually helped keep disadvantaged youths from getting involved in one of the regions other popular but more addictive exports. But what did I know? The tea was wrong too because it was harvested by poor kids who were paid with nothing more than a clip around the ear and a dose of cholera. In fact all the items in my kitchen were wrong because they came from large multinationals that exploited the poor and vulnerable and killed the polar bears. She stated she was a woman of principle and could not be a part of this world wide exploitation or contribute to the collateral damage caused by big business in their quest for profit. This principle obviously didn't stretch to the Gucci hand bag she carried or the iPhone that beeped and bonged relentlessly throughout the meal. Earlier I saw her looking at my wallpaper with strained look on her face. I thought maybe she didn't like the pattern or maybe it was trapped wind. I couldn't be sure. I now believe it was because she suspected I had stuck the paper on the wall with the tears of abandoned orphans and whale blubber instead of the conventional paste. Which in any case probably would have been wrong too.

After dinner we moved away from the killing field that was the kitchen and sat in the garden. Even this was was wrong because my garden shed was not sourced from an ecologically sustainable forest and because of this all the birds would suffocate, the seas would rise and the world would end. It would all be my fault, how could I be so irresponsible and ignorant?

No matter what the subject Jessica had an opinion on it and she was simply right. Money was wrong, the rich were evil, and big business and their leaders were like Hitler and the Third Reich. Criminals were misunderstood and oppressed. They simply needed a hug and they would change their ways. By now I was more than irritated.

Frank had hardly said a word all night and was currently nose deep in his second bottle of wine but he nearly choked on his Merlot when I casually dropped Jimmy Saville into the conversation. I realise that this is probably not an acceptable topic for polite dinner conversation but I was irritated and tired of being told I was wrong on everything without any sort of reasoned debate. Having got everyone's attention I asked if she really believed that her approach of hugging monsters like Saville would have meant they would have suddenly changed their ways and turned into normal decent human beings. Would animals like Fred West, Harold Shipman, Peter Sutcliffe or Jeffery Epstein have been model citizens if they had just been given a hug and asked not to do it again? I think not. Jessica struggled with this concept and concluded that I was being obstreperous.

Undeterred, I continued by asking about her recycled Prada shoes, biodegradable Gucci bag and her organic iPhone but it was lost on her. Then she hit me with it. She said I simply wasn't "woke". This is a word I've begun to hear recently. Apparently it means you have had your eyes opened to all the worlds social, economic and environmental problems. A sort of road to Damascus type moment. It's a trendy term for trendy people. You can look back through history and see people being woken up left right and centre and long before it was ever trendy.

You could certainly say the Suffragette movement was woke, so was Martin Luther King and you could probably even say the French Revolution was a woke event but then again is beheading a step too far? I fear that people like Jessica are diluting the suffering and persecution people have endured and are making a mockery of those who genuinely are trying to make a real difference to help those in need. Learning that McDonalds will now serve you carrots in a little bag directly through your Porsche window certainly doesn't qualify as being woke.

I have a lot of admiration for those who stand up and fight for what they believe to be right or to defend those that can't defend themselves. What I can't stand are frauds and charlatans and that is exactly what Jessica appeared to be. She was woke purely because it looks good on her instagram. She spouted her rhetoric and criticised all those around her but her principles went out the window when it came to her expensive shoes and must have technology. When it came time to leave, she certainly didn't have a problem plonking her backside on what used to be the backside of a cow. The animal had been peeled and washed simply so she would have a nice place to sit in her top of the range Range Rover. I get the feeling that when being woke is no longer trendy she will go back to sleep. She will move on to the next big thing, forgetting about all those deeply important and emotive issues that she never really cared about anyway.

This then is why you haven't eaten an After Eight since 1998. It is simply too much hassle to cater for all people's tastes these days. It's much simpler to off load this hassle to a professional restauranteur. The dinner party is dead and it's not coming back anytime soon. The little chocolate mint was simply the collateral damage of people waking up.

Don't worry, I will never utter the term "woke" again.

We Don't Need No Education

I doubt Pink Floyd were fortune tellers or time travellers from the future but how else could they have known how apt the above lyric could be when applied to the youth of today?

Somewhere along the line it has become fiercely fashionable to be stupid. Why this is truly baffles me but it seems to be everywhere. The youth of today appear to know nothing of the world around them or how to construct a meaningful sentence without the use of the word "like"or "literally" inexplicably thrown in half a dozen times. Like literally what is that all about?

I first noticed this creeping in years ago when something called reality TV first became popular. This was a turning point in television history. In an office or trendy bistro somewhere in the 90's, an ambitious TV executive in a shiny suit and hair to match, decided it would be a great money making idea to unleash uneducated arseholes into our living rooms. Unfortunately these morons became role models for society. It's been downhill ever since. How could the well meaning TV executive have foreseen the impact their decision would have on the future of humanity?

Now it's cool to be the colour of a radioactive tangerine.   Have blindingly white and unrealistically straight teeth the likes of which should only be viewed through prescription strength sunglasses and to swagger about with the most vacant clueless look on your face.   A look that now has somehow managed to infiltrate the Oval Office.

Ask an average teenager these days about the worlds capital cities or to do a simple calculation (without a calculator) and you will be met with shoulder shrugs and a series of "I don't knows." A recent conversation with the youngest girl child who incidentally is currently taking driving lessons, revealed that she believed a journey from Ireland to Germany could be carried out exclusively by road. "Like, why would you need a boat?   Cus there's literally no seas between Ireland and Germany, sure like it's all Europe, like" she professed. Not only did this highlight a lack of basic geography it also gives the impression that there was no understanding of the blitz, the Luftwaffe, the Battle of Britain or what the channel tunnel actually was buried under. Even the Irish Sea was missing from her knowledge.

Now I know she knows better than this but she seemed to be taking the line I described earlier. You might know the answer but don't dare tell anyone incase they assume you're intelligent. That's just not cool.

It might be tempting to lay all the blame for this at the orange webbed footed cast of TOWIE, Geordie Shore or whatever but I don't think thats the whole story. Technology has to shoulder some of the blame too. Why would you need to know anything when you can simply "google it".

That leads nicely onto my issues with the internet. If you are under 20, chances are you don't know a world without the internet, mobile phones or social media but then thats progress for you. The youth of today panic if the wifi disappears or their phone dies for the briefest of moments. They will never know the joy of leaving the house and being utterly unreachable. I don't believe that kids these days could cope without being tethered to the World Wide Web. They will never know the inconvenience of not having a 10p to use a public pay phone or the joy of watching a film in the cinema without a stream of god damn ringing, bleeps or clicks interspersed throughout the main feature. They will never be able to eat a meal without having to first photograph it from 8 angles to post on Instaface or take a picture of a stunning piece of scenery without having it ruined by their own pouty duck face pose.

I realise I'm in danger of giving you the impression that I dislike modern technology. You are probably imagining that I would be quite content to live in the retro shade of the 1980s, listening to cassette tapes on my walkman while eagerly awaiting the advent of the compact disc. You're probably right up to a point. Life was for the most part less complicated then, but then again I might be reminiscing through rose tinted glasses.

Modern technology is great, if it is used correctly. The internet can be a great learning tool but too many people can spend hours scrolling through Instatwit or Facegram looking at nonsense that has no bearing on your life whatsoever. Social media is a big source of grumpiness, in fact I think it deserves a chapter all of its own.

Doctors are fond of putting you through a treadmill test to see if your heart and lungs can cope with everyday activities without exploding through your chest cavity. A more accurate way to test your resolve is to try and have a conversation with a teenager. I guarantee your stress levels will reach heights previously unknown to science. Do you remember the comedy characters Kevin and Perry, the spotty, moody, spoilt adolescents brought to life by Harry Enfield and Kathy Burke? If not I strongly urge you to look them up. First time I saw them I thought it was a very funny show, I now realise it was so much more. It was a documentary, a warning and a disturbing insight to my future life.

Don't get me wrong. It would be inaccurate to lay the blame for all this solely at the feckless feet of todays youth. This is a multigenerational thing. My parents probably thought the same thing about my generation and their parents probably thought the same of them. The question is if each generation is genuinely getting progressively dumber, what will be the outcome in 100 years time? Will we become the modern equivalent of the Neanderthal? Roaming the earth etching out a mediocre existence through laziness and apathy, communicating only in a series of grunts and simple picture like symbols while avoiding all eye contact, but with perfectly straight white teeth and tangerine skin.

Oh wait...we may already be there..

Unrecognised Item In Bagging Area

Do you remember what it used to be like? You went to the supermarket loaded up your trolley with goods, went to the checkout, set your stuff onto a conveyer belt and the helpful operator scanned them. They even packed them into a bag for you.

Then at some point it changed. I think it started when an accountant decided that you should pack your own groceries to save the business time and money. Probably not a bad idea in itself but it has grown into the monster we have today. Now they want to take people out of the equation altogether. The self service checkout has arrived. You might think that after reading chapter 1 of this book I would be all for avoiding human contact when shopping. You would be correct but that is only the case when it's being replaced with something else that actually works and makes the whole experience simpler, quicker and less stressful.

Let me walk you through why these modern marvels of supermarket shopping make me grumpy.

Having trundled around the maze of aisles for an hour or so and retrieved all your basic needs for the next few days you decide that it is time to pay for your meagre collection of potatoes, pies and beans. Basket in hand you walk past several hundred empty and unmanned tills. Speed, convenience and penny pinching dictates that you now are forced to use what's called a self service checkout. You'll find them enclosed in a small pen, usually in a herd of 8 to 12. You are funnelled into the maelstrom at one end of the pen where you wait until a till becomes available. Of course your wait time is inevitably lengthened by the appearance of old Edna from chapter 1. She is at the front of the queue oblivious to the fact that a till has become available. She might as well be on Mars. Eventually reality sets in and she moves forward to begin the series of events that she inflicted in chapter 1.

In the interest of sanity we will skip forward to actually reaching the till. You're positioned in front of the screen, your basket is to your right and the dreaded "bagging area" is on your left.

You scan your first item and wait with bated breath for the beep. If you are lucky your item appears on the screen and you place the item in the bagging area. You repeat this several times and you think, "this is easy, I am a scanning genius" but wait, don't get carried away. Eventually an item just won't scan or worse still it scans and you place it in the bag but are immediately greeted with the condescending response "unexpected item in bagging area." Bollocks! You try and rearrange the bag, take the item out, put it back in again, hoping the computer will untangle itself and allow you to continue. The voice repeats its instruction in the same judgemental monotone manner. You feel the sweat break on your back as the eyes of the impatient shoppers behind you bore holes into your very soul. They are thinking the same thing you were just a few minutes ago when you had been stuck in the queue, but take comfort in the fact that in a few minutes they too will be reduced to a frustrated boiling mess.

Eventually the keeper of the tills appears beside you. They are the masters of the pen. This is their area, they are a God as far as you should be concerned. Invariably they are 16 to 18 years old, with a spotty face and speak in the typical teenage language of grunt. Of course there are exceptions to this, some of them actually can speak.

Armed with their Fob of Freedom and secret Code of Consent, they check you aren't pilfering products and unlock the till from its malfunction. Then with their head held high they swan off to continue their watch over their kingdom. Oh balls. The alcohol, scan it and wait for the return of the spotty teenager to check you are in fact old enough to drink the devils lemonade. There is nothing in this world more demeaning than being asked for ID by someone who until yesterday still wore nappies. Granted it has been a while since I've actually had to produce photographic evidence of my age. I think the last time was when I was attempting to buy a nice bottle of single malt at age 28 - my age not the whisky. Maybe I have a young face or they may actually have been legally blind, you can draw your own conclusion on that one but I didn't see a guide dog.

Anyway, while they are trying to size up your age you ask if the container your bottle is in has a security tag. A perfectly reasonable question as previous experience tells you there will be and you know those damn alarms will sound when you try to leave, prompting security to rifle through your shopping while you stand there looking like a common shoplifter.

Skipping forward to the point where everything is scanned and in the bag. Great, select your payment method and get out quick. Generally cards are straight forward but cash can present a problem for these hi tech machines. You can rest assured that half the notes in your wallet will be rejected forcing you to enter into a strange game of tug o war with a 20 quid note. You put it in and it spits it back out at you, you rotate it, flatten it, turn it back to front and upside down but it is to no avail. Your money is no good here. This is not your fault you have offered payment but you can't just leave or the constabulary will be called. In any case I don't think the argument that the machine said it was "on the house" would be a robust defence in court. So after much fiddling, cursing and fist clenching you eventually find acceptable cash and you are allowed to leave. Im not joking when I say I have witnessed grown men breakdown and cry while using these machines. It really is embarrassing for everyone involved when the trolley boy has to coax a middle-aged man out of the foetal position in the basket area and reunite him with his wife who, unwittingly sent the poor sap in to get a loaf of bread and pint of milk.

All of this could be avoided if it was left in the hands of a professional but in the interests of efficiency and cost effectiveness it must take longer.

Beep Beep Beep....Whats that?   A bloody a security tag. Step this way sir. Bollocks.

The Lycra Clad Menace

I realise a chapter on cyclists may be controversial. They seem to be everywhere these days, you could be sitting next to a secret cyclist right now. Take a good look at the people around you, you never know where they may be lurking and more disturbingly they have recently developed a militant wing.

When I was young, people had bikes. They were recreational items used for joy, pleasure and relaxation. As a kid I spent hours and hours on my bike. For me going out on a bike was as normal as putting on shoes and it wasn't just me, gangs of kids hung out on bikes everyday. Parents would actually put their kids out of the house to play on their bikes just to get them off the Nintendo or whatever. Have you heard a parent lately instruct their child to get out of the house and go play with the traffic on a two wheeled leg breaker?

Cycling now has transformed into an enthusiasts activity. Nothing will kill off an activity or take the fun out of it more than when the enthusiast get involved. A bike was once something you used between having learnt to walk and waiting to learn to drive. It was never intended to be a long term mode of transport unless you couldn't afford a car in which case it was used out of necessity rather than desire.

To use a bike now you must dress in strange and embarrassingly tight outfits the likes of which you only ever saw in the low budget sci-fi movies of the 70s. Essentially it is a socially acceptable way of wearing your S&M gear in public. You also have to have the right shoes, tinted glasses, streamlined helmets, heart monitors and all manner of devices that can measure every aspect of your performance and thats before you get to the actual machine itself.

A bike used to be a simple combination of frame, wheels and handle bars. The biggest decision you had was to choose what colour you wanted. Now they are fully customisable, ultra light weight, made from the newest space age materials with sophisticated gearing and formula one standard brakes. Everything can be customised to get the best out of your cycling session. The most customisation I ever had on my bike was sticking cards in the spokes or adding a few stickers.

So you're all set up for your cycle, you've donned your lycra bodysuit and leave the house looking and thinking that you are in the Tour de France while your neighbours are thinking more along the lines of Tour de Farce.

Now I don't have anything against cyclists themselves. If you want to wear bright yellow lycra and look ridiculous then go for it, what you do in the privacy of your own home is entirely your business. My problem is that they insist on inflicting their interest on the rest of us normal road users. At least stamp collectors and train spotters have the decency to hide discreetly in the shadows.

Like a slow and badly driven car, a cyclist can be just as dangerous on the road. They need an extraordinary amount of room and create a wake of angry, frustrated drivers in their slipstream. They wobble frantically and unpredictably down the middle of the road under the illusion that they are Sir Bradley Wiggins. You sit behind at 20mph cursing and screaming while trying to get safely around this midlife crisis on wheels. Often they work in pairs and ride side by side making passing them an impossibility. It only gets worse if you are unfortunate enough to encounter one of the many cycling gangs that roam the countries roads. You only thought the Hells Angels were a menace, they have nothing on these lycra clad pedlars. If I had my way, you would only be allowed to have one of these serious bikes after completing a full 4000 mile trip over the Andes perched on top of a Penny Farthing. If after this you are still interested in bikes or indeed were still alive, then you will be allowed to dress in your lycra and resume your menacing ways on the road.

If you look carefully you will find this sort of enthusiast take over is happening with various other mundane activities. Take a look next time you go out of the house. You will see people out walking. They will seem normal enough but watch out. Amongst the normal wanderers you will find the walking cyclist equivalent. You will know them when you see them. They are dressed in what has become known as athleisure wear. Before now this stuff was only worn in the confines of a gym, now its on the streets. People are beginning to wear this gear for a simple walk. Take note they are likely wearing earphones and carrying a trendy water bottle. Now you may think, "ahh thats someone out jogging and they are suitably dressed for this" I have checked and almost all of them never break into anything that could even be loosely construed as a brisk walk. I urge you to heed my warning. In the not too distant future you will not be able to go for a simple walk as we know it. Much the same as you can't just hop on a bike and head to the shops anymore.

Life Is Rubbish

This is a problem that has been building for years but has really taken off recently. Before I launch into this I want to make it clear that I have nothing against protecting and maintaining the environment. I do believe climate change is a real thing and that we need to do our bit to preserve our planet. All those man eating creatures that live in the wilderness need to stay there, which they won't if we destroy their houses.

My issue is that the UK produces about 31 billion tonnes of rubbish each year, most of which seems to end up in my garden. I now have 5 rubbish bins for my waste. In fact a whole section of my garden that used to house just two bins, now resembles a midsized regional recycling plant.

Firstly I have a bin for food waste, one for paper and cardboard, one for garden waste, one for glass and plastic and one for everything else. I am spending hours everyday ankle deep in rubbish. I sort it, separate it and allocate it to the correct bin. You might think this is an exaggeration, but due to local authority cuts our bins are collected every two weeks if we are lucky and if a stray plastic bottle makes it into the wrong bin, they refuse to empty the whole thing and another two weeks worth of crap gathers around my house. Then you find yourself in the strange position of having too much rubbish for the refuse collection workers to collect. If the bin lid won't close they won't empty it, nor will they lift single rubbish bags either. I fear this is in some way linked to a health and safety official. This leaves you with two options, first you can load up your own car with the putrid collection of rubbish, dodge the lycra clad cyclists (see previous chapter) and transport it yourself to the local tip, leaving you to suffer the faint smells of rotting fish guts in your car for weeks to come.

Your second option is to curtail all rubbish accumulation until you can catch up. This is pretty much impossible unless you live on fresh air for two weeks, by which stage you will be too weak to get your rubbish to the curb for collection anyway. Neither of these options hold much appeal with me.

I remember a time when a friendly council employee in a donkey jacket would not only happily collect all your rubbish but would even come into your garden to retrieve your bin and then put it back after he had emptied it. I get the feeling now that we are very close to the stage where we will be responsible for loading our own rubbish directly into the bin lorry ourselves. The only thing stopping this is likely that health and safety guy with his clipboard and risk assessments from the nanny state.

I don't mind changing my old lightbulbs for LED versions that are cheaper to run. I think that pumping my cavity walls full of polystyrene or whatever is an excellent idea and switching off lights and electrical appliances when they are not in use is just common sense, but when it becomes inconvenient for me then i'm afraid thats where I have to draw the line.

You see I believe that most people try to do the right thing but guess what, everyone is lazy. That's why the country is blighted by fly tipping. People who are too lazy, feckless or stupid will happily load an old urine stained mattress into the back of a van and then, rather than drive 2 miles to the local dump, will drive 10 miles into the countryside and throw it over a hedge. Where is the logic in that? It's not just mattresses, mountains of bags full of normal household waste get dumped everyday in beauty spots simply because there is too much of it for people to be bothered to deal with.

In my opinion it would be better if all the plastic packaging and cardboard we seem to think we need these days was never produced in the first place. Even China now has too much of it and is refusing to accept the container ship loads of the stuff we used to pay them to take off our hands. Logically, why do we need to encase our onions in plastic that will last a thousand years longer than humanity itself when the item inside will be gone in less than a week?

Think for a second about all the unnecessary packaging you had from making your dinner today. If it didn't exist in the first place then you wouldn't need to spend an eternity sorting it, you wouldn't need 27 different bins to put all the non existent waste into and the bin man or bin man/woman's job would be easier. Everyone wins including the environment.

This leads onto a second issue I have with modern life. Things these days are no longer built to last but rather built to be replaced. When and why did this change? It used to be that when your washing machine stopped washing you called a local repairman. He came around, looked it over, had a cup of strong tea and after a fair amount of tutting and head shaking fixed the problem. Now you would struggle to find someone capable of fixing your leaky tap never mind an entire washing machine. Instead these items are discarded for even the most minor of faults and replaced with a new model with guess what... even more packaging than the last one had. Not to mention of course that most white goods are now made in the Far East, or at least their component parts are. These are then shipped, flown and hauled all around the world in all sorts of oil guzzling machines before they arrive in your kitchen and then promptly begin to disintegrate.

On a more local level, we have the plastic bag tax that came into law a few years ago. Now if you want to put your items into a plastic bag in order to get them home from the shops you will be charged 5p for each one you use. If I only have a few things to carry I will do without a bag, but if I have to struggle to get my produce to my cupboard without my onions falling on the floor I will gladly pay the cold hard cash for the convenience of a bag. However a problem has arisen from this tax that I fear has not yet been recognised. It is the evolution of the bag for life. The idea behind this, as I'm sure you are aware, is that you take this bag along with you when you go to do your shopping and use it over and over again. In theory this means fewer plastic bags are needed and the world will be saved. The problem is that I now have a drawer in my kitchen bulging with these things, my car is full of them too because I never remember to take one with me into the shop. I have hundreds of the things, if anything my consumption of plastic has skyrocketed. I have discussed this matter with a few others and it seems to be a common problem. I think the only ones benefiting from this whole thing are the manufacturers of the blasted things.

Im afraid this recycling lark seems to be a bit of a self fulfilling money racket. Let's do the world a favour and take a leap forward to 1950 when everything was wrapped in paper that simply rotted away.

Who The F**k Are You?

Having switched on my TV, or box of perpetual disappointment as I now call it, I was greeted by a fanfare of flashing lights and a shouty man insisting that I simply had to spend the next few weeks watching something called "Im a Celebrity, Get Me Out of Here."

If I was one of those weak willed, easily influenced mouth breathers (you know who you are) I probably would have been sucked into the premise that I would be a social outcast if I didn't tune in and engage with this farce. Thankfully I'm a social outcast anyway and more importantly I don't really care.

Luckily, like you I am a man of much stronger fortitude, and realised that spending an evening watching this rubbish would be about as enjoyable as having my eyelids stapled to the floor. So I switched off, but not before seeing the exciting line up of celebrities that would be worming their way into the nations homes over the next few weeks. I guarantee that most people watching all had the same thoughts, Who the f**k is that? What are they from? and isn't that

that bloke who played whats his face on that thing?

The more astute amongst you will know that this isn't just limited to the I'm a Celebrity branded show.   All these types of shows are the same, Strictly Come Dancing, Dancing on Ice, Celebrity Big Brother and all the other so called celebrity versions of what once had been fairly innocuous TV programmes.   They all started with the good idea that celebrities would draw in the masses. Their assumption was right however they failed to recognise that there are only so many celebrities alive and willing to degrade themselves to the extent required by some of these shows.   Generally they are all from the far end of the alphabet, A-Listers they are not.

Perhaps at this point I should try and clarify what a celebrity actually is.   According to the Collins English Dictionary a celebrity is defined as someone who is famous, especially in areas of entertainment such as films, music, writing , or sport. In other words a celebrity is someone who through a talent, skill or hard work has achieved recognition.   I do not think that very many of todays celebrities fit that bill. Now you can be a celebrity by simply being watched watching TV and making vaguely bland and stupid statements. (see previous section ref. dumb being cool). Gone are the days when you could switch on your TV and be greeted by a genuinely talented singer, actor, writer or comedian. You have to search very hard to find the shining diamonds amongst the sea of has beens, wannabes and attention seekers that wash up in your front room these days.

The problem however is not confined to your TV. If you have logged onto your internet machine lately you will no doubt have come across something called Tik Tok. I don't have the sum of a horologists notion what this thing is or why it appeals to anyone, but the young and informed seem to like it very much. As far as I can tell, all it involves is a spot of minor epilepsy while miming along to a song. Some people are so good at it they have become celebrities in their own right, apparently. I remember a time when lip syncing was considered a major performance faux pas and you were widely and ferociously ridiculed and quite rightly too. Miming was the refuge of Britney Spears, Ashlee Simpson (who?) and strange French men trapped in boxes who had an unhealthy interest in face painting. I fear the world has now gone beyond the point of no return. Time could be better spent actually learning to sing properly. If this proves unsuccessful then by all means sing your heart out into a hairbrush but do it like people used to, in the privacy of their own bedroom without the internet watching.

Celebrity Tv shows, miming and reality nonsense aside I feel that TV has become a bastion of blandness. I love a good comedy but they just don't seem to make them anymore. The great shows of the past, Only Fools and Horses, Fawlty Towers, Monty Python, the Carry On series, Porridge and MASH are all gone. They have been replaced with cheap laughs and unintelligent coarse humour. Films such as Ghostbusters, National Lampoons and Police Academy (only the early ones, the later ones are just silly) are relegated to the echoes of time, forgotten by most and ignored by the young. I urge you to hunt through you movie collection and revisit the tv shows and films of your youth and I guarantee the rush of nostalgia and laughter will bring more joy to your heart than anything on TV now.

If you are like me you probably still think of John Cleese running his dysfunctional hotel on the

English Riviera, Alan Alda as Hawkeye Pierce still lives in the Swamp in South Korea and Del Boy and Rodney are still wheeling and dealing from Nelson Mandela House. In your head they are as they were. Their world does not change, they play on a continuous loop as they live out their lives in little boxes in the cupboard under your stairs. They will always be there as a steadfast rock to cling to in this fast changing world.

A word of warning though, do not be tempted to look up any of your favourite actors from the past. You will find that most have not faired well over time, who has? Or worse still some will be dead. Your heart will sink and you will be left with that shuddering empty, sorrowful feeling that you get when you realise times have changed and things are no longer as they once were.

I suspect that in the future todays youth will think exactly the same about their heroes, that is if any of todays celebrities hang around long enough to have a legacy worth remembering. I'd certainly find it hard to shed a misty tear over the likes of Keith Essex or Joey Lemon.

Insignificant Politics

If there is one sure way to cause controversy and build divisions politics is it. Next to religion it is the one true divider of people.

Where I am from politics is a byword for confusion, deception, ineptitude, scandal, fraud and bullshit. I'm sure whatever country you live in you will likely come to the same conclusion. In my complicated little corner of the world we have not had a functional government since it collapsed well over two years ago. From what I can tell it seems to have fallen apart because someone left the heat on and ran up a big bill. The opposition took umbrage to this and threw their toys out of the pram. Everyone else saw this as a good idea and decided to throw their toys out too and then everyone set about arguing who should pick them up first. Thats the main overview, but it bores me to death and if you are not from where I am, you will have no idea or interest in the tedium that was the Renewable Heat Incentive scandal, so I'll move on.

The slightly wider outlook only gets more depressing. Brexit. It pains me to even type it. Even the mere suggestion of the B word makes me cringe. The whole debacle is embarrassing, frustrating and an utter waste of everyones time. Even without this whole fiasco, politics appears to me to be a collection of overpaid time wasters, shouting and slinging well spoken insults at each other all with the apparent aim of running the country and getting things done. The only thing that these blundering buffoons excel at is having an outstanding ability to avoid giving a straight answer to any question put to them. I suspect that if any of us took that approach to our jobs we would be sacked and standing in line at the unemployment office by 11 o'clock on Monday morning. I try to treat politicians much in the same way I treat a violent bout of unexpected watery flatulence. With extreme care, considered scepticism and plausible deniability. This approach has stood me well so far and I see no requirement to alter my view.

If we take a look further afield we find that politics and the business of running a country only gets stranger. Our friends in America seem to have confused their presidential elections with some sort of talent show and now they've ended up with a Trump in the White House. Incidentally to us in the UK a trump is something very different. To us having a Trump in the White House would be considered a monumental social gaffe. Then again "The Donald" as he likes to be called is a bit of a social hand grenade.

Then we have Trumps new best friend in the Far East who likes intercontinental missiles but seems to have no interest whatsoever in his hair style or human rights. Further north we have the ex KGB agent riding topless on horses and who allegedly runs a secret service that has a keen interest in Anglican Cathedrals and poison umbrellas, allegedly. Incidentally the last major wall that was built was in Germany with big help from the Russians. In fact it's reported that Vladimir Putin himself was stationed there in his early days. Maybe Trump could ask him to help get his wall off the ground.... oh wait no maybe thats not such a good idea. Anyway Hasselhoff would only knock it down again, though I think the only reason the wall was brought down was due to a concerted public effort on both sides to stop him from singing on top of it.

Anyway I digress. Moving west from the Russians we have the middle east which is pretty much just a convoluted mess of religions, treaties, fragile ceasefires and sand.

Europe is unsure of its direction and is so bogged down in bureaucracy its like a dwarf struggling to keep 27 plates spinning on top of 27 sticks that are just slightly taller than his reach while riding a unicycle, blindfolded.

Africa has some nice spots but has a bit of famine, many local wars, lots of mad dictators, lashings of corruption and some Ebola. South America has drugs, gangs, cartels, corruption and some more mad dictators. The Artic and Antarctic are melting and will soon be gone and Australia is upside down and mostly on fire.

On top of all that the world is apparently teetering on the brink of another financial crisis that will make the last one look about as serious as a 5 year olds piggy bank falling over.

You may have gathered that over the years I have been somewhat disillusioned by politics, world events and the people apparently in charge of the whole thing. You may be thinking that politics matters and is vitally important to each and every one of us. But consider the following statistics.

The Moon is 400,000 km from earth

Mars is the closest planet to us and is a mere 78,000,000 km away from earth.

Neptune is only 4,350,000,000 km away.

1 light year is about 9,500,000,000,000 km

Its 27,700 light years to the centre of our own galaxy and 2,900,000 light years to our nearest Galaxy Andromeda.

Are things in perspective yet?

Our sun is just one of at least 100 billion stars in the Milky Way and each of these have countless planets spinning around them that we know nothing about and they probably know nothing of us. In fact if the earth was to be snuffed out of existence tomorrow it would have about the same impact on our galaxy as you removing just one grain of sand from all of earths beaches and deserts combined. If all that wasn't enough, if all of time was represented by the room you are sitting in now, all of human existence wouldn't even reach past the layer of dust under the sofa.

With all the vastness of space and the insignificance of this tiny planet and the people on it, does Mr Johnson's Brexit, Trumps wall, or a mad Koreans firework collection seem overly important?   Probably not but then again the distance to the moon doesn't affect the price of my Custard Creams but the economic distance from Brussels just might.

Maybe the solution is to round up all the politicians, warlords and dictators on earth and blast them off into space. If they survive the 2.54 million year trip to Andromeda they can argue and shout at each other as much as they want. They can build walls and fire as many missiles as they like. At least we won't have to listen to them and the world might just be a safer place.

Farting Fifties

You may find it strange for me to include money as something that makes me grumpy. Having previously written two short books on money and personal finance you'd probably think that I would love money. You'd be right, who in their right mind doesn't like money? It allows you to live, buy nice things, go on holidays and buy clothes to cover your ageing body. No one will complain about that.

No. Money is not the issue here. What is the issue is the many forms it now takes. I like having a crisp £10 note in my pocket, going to the shop and exchanging it for a few essentials, like Mars bars or something. This sort of transaction has gone on for hundreds and hundreds of years, but now it's changing.

You can use debit or credit cards, they have been around for ages and I like them. They are as simple and as easy as cash. What I don't like are all the other ways to pay now. Pay with your mobile or watch or why not pay using a handy app? I once witnessed a guy try to buy petrol using a new app on his phone. It didn't work, he just stood there on the forecourt mindlessly tapping his phone, looking more and more distraught. Eventually he gave up, went inside and joined the back of the queue with the rest of us plebes. Anyway isn't there signs up in petrol stations specifically telling you not to use your phone near the pumps?

Now you can even pay for things using bitcoin. BITCOIN, my god don't get me started on Bitcoin. I once spent a couple of hours eating dinner with a bloke who was adamant that I should liquidate all my assets, sell all my possessions and put it all into Bitcoin. It was the next big thing, it will make you richer quicker than anything else out there. He was right but it would also have made me very poor very quickly too. It was something that I never even considered doing. Not because I had some crystal ball that could tell the future and certainly not because I knew anything about it, at the time I had barely even heard of cryptocurrency. No, what made my mind up was the conversation that had preceded this advice.

Let me set the scene for you. It was about 7pm on a mildly pleasant Wednesday evening in early 2014. The restaurant was dimly lit with industrial style mood lighting, hipster style decorations adorned the exposed brick walls and nondescript beige infused music floated on top of the smell of freshly baked bread and seafood avocado chowder. Sitting across from me at the table was the other half, and on either side of us sat two of my best friends that I've known for nearly twenty years, in fact we shared a house together during the university days. Opposite them sat their respective partners. At the end sat the crypto guy. He was introduced to us and he seemed friendly. A typical modern older student type, quirky and not yet ground down by the harsh realities of real life, stuck somewhere between student and adult life but not really wanting to commit fully to either.

After we ordered our starters conversation began to flow. Now bear in mind, I had never met this guy before, but no sooner had my battered mushrooms with garlic dressing and side salad landed in front of me, I was being introduced to the concept that everything I knew was wrong and that the earth was flat. Yes, you read that right. Bitcoin Boy as I came to call him firmly believed that the earth was FLAT and with all the conviction of a Jehovah's Witness extremist he was trying to convert me.

Obviously this man was mad. It was 2014AD not 14BC. Opening a conversation with some dubious theory that the earth was as flat as the piece of slate my mushrooms were being served on does not inspire confidence, so naturally I treated everything that was said after that with an appropriate degree of scepticism.

His proclamations that the earth was flat was the equivalent of your boss calling you to his office for a right old fashioned chewing out, he may even be about to sack you, but as he opens his mouth he lets rip the most tremendous flat earth shattering fart. Now he is done for, nothing he can say after that can even be taken remotely seriously. All credibility is lost.

Warren Buffett is worth billions and billions of dollars and is regarded as one of the most successful investors that ever lived but if he was to offer me sound financial advice moments after letting one rip, it would put him on par with that guy at school who ate his own bogies. Unless he was farting £50 notes I'm not interested.

This is why I can never, ever put any credibility into bitcoin or any other new fangled payment methods or crypto whatnots. To me it's all a bit flat and farty.

Influenced By a Bucket of Horse Crap

Advertising has been around for thousands of years. The ancient Egyptians use papyrus for advertising. Historic businessmen and entrepreneurs could pin their adverts to the pyramid walls like an ancient exchange and mart. Cavemen probably used crude drawings on walls to sell their woolly mammoth jumpers. Pretty much as long as people have been around, advertising in some form or other hasn't been far behind and I think that is great. Human ingenuity and the desire to build and progress is necessary, if we didn't have that we would still be sitting in caves and wearing a peeled woolly mammoth to keep warm.

The Caxton press introduced to England in 1476 by William Caxton arguably launched the printed advertisement to the masses and it has been big business ever since. We are constantly bombarded from all angles with invitations to buy and advertisers have become more and more creative and sneaky. Now you can be advertised to without even realising it. The whole thing has become so saturated and degraded that an entire culture has been born out of it. Im talking about the influencers. These people irritate me on an unprecedented scale. I'm sure some of them are very nice well meaning people but would you trust them? Would you trust anyone involved primarily in advertising/selling? They are the modern day internet equivalent of a used car salesman.

Technology bores out new jobs all the time and old jobs fade into the cobwebbed halls of history. When we used to travel around on horseback a man would be employed to pick up what fell out of the back of the animal and put it in a bucket. Now with the internet we have social media influencers. In the old days the more horses you followed and the bigger your bucket the more money you made. Im sure some of the biggest crap lifters of the past made a reasonable living from it. Now the more followers you have on social media and the more crap you can peddle to them the more money you can make. Some of them make millions of pounds from it. However what credentials do these people have? Do they actually believe in the products they are desperately promoting or are they willing to promote just about anything in return for a few quid or a few free samples or handouts?

I recently saw an article about a young woman who's name and face escape me but she identifies herself as a social media influencer. This is her career, her business and her livelihood. Nothing wrong with that, make your living whatever way you see fit. What I found hilariously funny was when her business model failed, essentially she kicked over her steaming bucket of crap and her horse bolted.

It seems that being an influencer with so many thousands of followers entitled her to ask for free stuff and in return she would speak kindly about any company or product that took her up on her offer. This model must have worked reasonably well, that is until valentines day arrived. She decided that she and her significant other would like to spend a romantic weekend away. Perfectly reasonable you might say, i'd do the same myself. Except she didn't just choose a hotel she liked, booked a room and paid the way you or I would. No, what she appears to have done is pen a generic email detailing her sphere of influence in cyberspace and how it would be in the hotels best interest if they allowed her to stay, free of charge over valentines and in return she would say nice things about them. This she apparently spammed this out to many hotel email addresses in the hope that one might be caught unaware and yield to her demands.

When I read this story I immediately thought of one of those old style gangster movies where two guys in pinstripe suits walk into some poor saps office and tell him they can protect his business because you know "accidents" can happen, meanwhile the other guy casually starts breaking things in a nonchalant manner.

Thankfully this apparent extortion attempt was thwarted when a quick thinking Irish hotelier made public his reply to her request. In short he told her where to get off and he pulled no punches. He explained that he could not possibly tell his staff that they would not get paid for washing her dishes or cleaning her sheets or attending to her every whim because instead they would get a mention on this woman's insta face video. He pointed out the fact that his hotel business had many social media followers too and he really didn't see how her free weekend would benefit anyone but her.

Of course when the funny Irish man made this letter public he was rightly praised by most but ridiculed by others. Our influencer, having been slated for her unashamed blagging attempt, tried to control the damage by making a tearful video explaining that she didn't mean any harm, she hadn't done anything wrong and that this is the way the world of business worked these days. Strangely this only made things worse.

She became a bit of a poster girl for the so called snowflake generation. Numerous videos popped up in reply to her, most of which explained that in fact money is how business works and not favours. When goods and services are supplied it is on the understanding that a monetary reimbursement will be provided for said goods or service. Many people pointed out that she was just making a scene, she tried to blag a free weekend away, it didn't work move on. You are entitled to nothing and you should pay your way like everyone else.

I followed this story for weeks and I took great amusement from it. It encapsulated many things that I see wrong with the world today. Many people today feel they are entitled to everything and god forbid that anyone should tell them otherwise because the so called snowflake melts in the heat of rejection. It used to be that anyone who went around blagging free stuff or making a living by taking advantage of others was called a con artist. I guess things change but I'm not sure I want to live in a world in which being Social Media Influencer is deemed a real job. Of course it's not beyond the realms of possibility that this whole fiasco could have been engineered as an elaborate publicity stunt in itself, who knows? Perhaps it's all smoke and mirrors but that's just the cynic in me.

Maybe if I mention Virgin Galactic, Sir Richard will fly me to the moon on his spaceship, complementary of course.

Zombie Nation

The pharmaceutical business is big business. Everyone will need some form of medication at some point in their lives. It might be a little vitamin tablet or a cancer beating dose of chemotherapy but there can be no doubt that drugs save lives. We have come a long way since 1928 when Alexander Fleming sneezed into a Petri dish and discovered penicillin. It was only in 1861 that Louis Pasteur first postulated that germs might exist. Before that people thought they got sick for all sorts of reasons, you might be possessed by evil spirits, maybe you had been guilty of some misdemeanour and a disappointed God was dishing out some much deserved vengeance. Or maybe you were just unlucky. In actual fact the vast majority of people got sick because of poor hygiene. The microscopic world of bacteria and viruses thrived in an as yet undiscovered world.

The Black death that devastated Europe in the mid 1300s and wiped out up to half the population was a complete mystery at the time and all sorts of reasons were put forward for its cause. The King of France looked to the stars for answers believing that the conjunction of three planets caused the problem, as it turns out rats in conjunction with the fleas they carry pay very little attention to astrology.

Since then most people have come to realise that astrology is utter twaddle and reserved exclusively for the stupid, the gullible and the insane.   Science has taken over and the development of pharmaceutical drugs have saved millions of lives several times over but it is a relatively new development.   The recreational drug business has been going much longer.

It is rumoured that some liberal Sumerians loved a hit of Opium as early as 5000B.C.   The Egyptians started brewing alcohol in 3500B.C and Napoleon brought a load of cannabis back to France in 1800.   An act that if you attempted now would surely be your Waterloo.   We can safely deduce that throughout human history large swaths of the population must have been totally off their heads and thats before the hippies of the 60s got involved.

So we have established that human civilisation has had its fair share of crackheads, crackpots and consciousness expanders.   This trait is unlikely to change in the future but what makes me concerned is the type of drug used today. Some people take drugs today like they are sweets and we are not talking your casual spliff or acid tab here, we are talking about serious mass produced, chemically engineered, highly concentrated prescription drugs. You only have to look at our nations prisons to get an idea of the problem. Her Majesty would simply not be amused. The hippies are long gone and have taken their flowers and messages of peace and love with them. The tie-dye generation has been replaced by the pill munching zombie generation who as far as I can tell have no agenda or coherent message whatsoever.

The sixties left us with an image of chilled, spaced out nonthreatening rainbow painting tree huggers who came in peace with free love and good karma, man.

In those days the cannabis and LSD trend was tied tightly with the peace and love movement. It even had its own music. The cannabis was cultured as was the culture of cannabis. Even the dance music movement of the nineties had love inducing ecstasy as their drug of choice. Today youngsters are simply taking the most bizarre and harmful concoction of substances known to man and as far as I can tell this has no link to any cultural or popular movement. Powerful tablets and psychoactive substances today can create a scene from the Walking Dead better than any Hollywood special effects department could. There have been instances reported that involved people being disembowelled and eaten by a face munching cretin off their own face on what's called Alpha-PVP also known as Flakka or bath salts. This is not made by Radox to aid relaxation after a tough day at the office, it is a powerful amphetamine based synthetic drug that simply seems to turn its user into an uncontrollable monster. Why anyone would want to ingest such a substance is beyond me.

The kids these days seem to just want to use drugs to mash up their brains. The creativity and passion has gone leaving behind a vile scummy residue thats prone to violence, greed and indifference. Thats very far removed from the mind expanding and creative aims of the Beatles or the Rolling Stones. The Fab 4 gave us a Walrus and a Yellow Submarine with cannabis and sunshine acid. Todays drug users look more like they have been attacked by a walrus and had a submarine fall on them. It really is depressing.

Taking some of the stuff available today is the equivalent of putting your brain through a food mixer. In fact putting your head in a blender might actually be less harmful to your health.

If you don't believe me or have not witnessed the blight caused by the misuse of substances such as Xanax and whats known as Spice, please type either of these drug names into your Youtube followed by the word zombie. I guarantee the videos you will see will simultaneously be the funniest and most depressing thing you will ever witness. The people you will see would struggle to say their own name never mind pen, arrange and record a multi million pound album. Then again if the nation is generally dumbing down then the prevailing drugs of choice will reflect that.

I doubt in 50 years people will look back at the use of these drugs as fondly or with the same strange affection that the sixties enjoy. Then again John Lennon had rose tinted glasses, maybe we're looking at history the same way.

Grim Reaper Protection

You have probably noticed, or at least you will now that it has been pointed out to you, that almost every TV advert today is trying to sell you protection from something or compensation for something else. For the past 4 years I have had the same friendly and concerned man appear in my living room every half hour to ask why I have not yet claimed for being miss sold Payment Protection Insurance. Stern people in suits enquire every 15 minutes if I have been injured in an accident that wasn't my fault. I haven't, at least not since they asked me in the last commercial break. I didn't realise walking to the kitchen and putting the kettle on could be so fraught with danger that I'd need a team of lawyers on constant standby. I can take some solace in the fact that these companies have paid lots of money to be on my TV a million times a day but I cannot forgive the bastard that rings me up everyday at the most inconvenient moments to chat to me about the accident he is convinced I have been involved in. It must cost him a fortune to call from India everyday at peak times.

Sometimes I play along and ask a few questions myself. Give him the impression he is on the cusp of success. Encourage him and thank him for taking the time out of their busy day to call you. You can hear the excitement in their voice as they believe they might actually have a customer hooked on the other end of their line. String it along for as long as you can but when it gets to the point where they are asking for personal information, start to spe k in bro en up wo ds as if the sig al i re ly bad. Enjoy the manic frustration they are now experiencing as their one potential customer slips away, then blast them full pelt with a rendering of Johnny Cash's Hurt or similar sorrowful tune of your choice. Providing it is sad and melancholy enough it will induce a complete breakdown. Then hang up and return to what you were doing before you were so rudely interrupted, safe in the knowledge that you have succeeded in making someone else's day just a little bit worse. This can continue everyday until they are fed up with the whole charade and simply stop calling.

All this frivolity aside there is a more serious problem afoot. It comes in the form of an advert that has become as prevalent as the ambulance chasing solicitors. I know what you're thinking but it is not the payday loan sharks. You'll know this advert when you see it, there are several different versions of it but they all have the same grim message. YOU ARE GOING TO DIE!

Yes, the funeral protection racket is alive and well. Now these bunch of coffin chasers really irritate me. I'm sitting at home on a Friday evening after a hard weeks work. I've just had my dinner, got tidied up and decided to put my feet up and pour myself a wee dram of single malt and think about absolutely nothing. All is right with the world. Then the bastards strike. A cheerful scene greets you on the screen, a grandfather kicking football with his grandson, a husband and wife strolling happily along a forest walk or two fresh faced pensioners sitting in armchairs reading the papers together or doing the crossword without a care in the world. The colour drains from the screen, Grandads gone. Doom, gloom and despair surround those left behind like a thick fog, but it's not the loss of the cheery old fella that has them upset. No, they're upset because the bloody funeral has to be paid for and the selfish old git made no provision for life's inevitable outcome. Now my weekend is ruined, I am going to die. Bollocks.

Im not upset about my eventual demise, realistically it happens to everyone at some stage. The biggest fact of life is in fact death, but I have that thought pushed right the way to the back of my mind, buried somewhere under the memory of birthdays, anniversaries, tax returns and outstanding bills that need paid. Hopefully those around me will shed a tear when the time comes for me to shake off this mortal coil but I hope it is because I'm now worm feed and not because they have to pay the bloke who dug the hole to put me in.

Back to the depressed people in the advert. A friend usually appears at this stage and puts a gentle hand on the bereaved woman's shoulder and reminds them that actually the dead guy had been paying £3 a week since he turned 50 and they can now pay out up to £5000 to help cover the cost of the funeral. The colour returns to the miserable scene and it turns into one of those happy scenes from Mary Poppins or the likes. Then comes the stern warning, "Don't leave your family to pay for your funeral after you've gone, take out a funeral protection plan with (insert trustworthy friendly corporate name here) and have the peace of mind that they will be looked after when you've gone"

Now I'm sitting here thinking, how long have I got left? If I take out one of these plans and I die after 2 years I'll get value for money. If I stick around for another 40 years I'll have paid them way too much. It's a conundrum that I think can be solved very simply. Do nothing.

The average life expectancy at present is well into the eighties and getting higher with medical developments and better healthcare. So after a good 80 years on this earth if you haven't been able to scrape together the means to cater for your own demise or there isn't enough in your estate to cover it then the question must be asked, what have you been doing all this time?

Anyway why should I pay for my own funeral, I'm dead, its not like I can even enjoy the day out. I'll be unconscious in the box and I bet I won't even be offered a ham sandwich or a wee dram at the wake.

These people should stop tormenting all those people who will only die once. If they had true foresight and any business acumen they should instead focus on those that subscribe to the idea of reincarnation. Think about the return business.

No Need For Water, The Fire Is All But Out

A common gripe us older folk have often involves music or rather what actually passes for music these days. It would be very easy to sit here and lambast all modern music as terrible and crap but that would be unfair. There has always been terrible and crap music. 93% of music created in the 80s proves this theory. It is possible to find good music these days, you just have to wade through an enormous amount of talentless dribble to find it.

Even when Beethoven was rocking out his 5th symphony in C minor, there must have been composers who made rubbish songs and were rightly ridiculed for it and maybe even accused of heresy for their works. Was there a Top of the Baroques in the 1600s? If so, I bet Cliff Richard was on it.

Every decade has had their iconic bands some even last through multiple decades. Take the last 50 years or so. The musical landscape is littered with big names and big talent like Elvis, Bob Dylan, The Beatles, The Sex Pistols, U2,

Springsteen and Nirvana. I fear that today we are approaching anything but nirvana. I doubt very many of the current X Factor winners will still be churning out or selling hits after 2 or 3 years never mind 10 or 20.

It's not just the calibre of the artists or musicians that seems to have plummeted, the standard of lyrics now fall way short when compared to the likes of Dylan, Bowie or Jagger. A young chap that goes by the name of Drake seems to be popular, at least this week anyway. I heard some of his songs on the wireless and I've noticed that they seem to be lacking in anything that could be described as having depth or indeed substance. One in particular called "Hotline Bling" I believe, is a prime example of this. He spends 4 minutes 11 seconds describing how a lady used to call him on his cell phone. After listening to 2 minutes of the thing I wanted to take his cell phone and shove it where the music doesn't shine.

They say that music often reflects the times we live in. It is a reactionary medium, an outlet for passion, protest and emotion. In the past bands like The Clash, The Rolling Stones and The Sex Pistols wrote songs in protest at poverty, the Vietnam war, politics and oppressive regimes around the world. Now we have well groomed dudes with their bling lamenting how some woman used to call them from time to time on a mobile phone. It has all got a bit wishy washy for my liking.

Now you may be thinking who are you to sit in judgement over what is proper music and what is not. Well, let me tell you. Firstly I have fully functioning ears and secondly, around the time I was due to leave the protective institution that was school, I decided to bin the idea of continuing on the expected path of a boring business degree and instead spent 4 years studying Music Production. I'm glad I did. It was some of the best, most character forming years of my life. Aside from learning the theory and practicalities of the music business, a whole world of music as yet unknown to me was revealed.

Undoubtably the most influential part of these years came from the people I met. They were some of the most interesting and eclectic people you could ever hope to meet. From scruffy, unkempt and next to homeless guitar players to an exquisitely eccentric retired solicitor who was working through his bucket list. It was exciting times. I loved every second of it, if I could I would go back and do it all over again. I felt alive, like I was doing something outside of the norm, against the stuffy system. Then life took over again. The party was nice while it lasted but thats all it was, a party.

I realise now that dreams die, people change and life marches on but way down deep inside that spark still exists. It lies there waiting for the opportunity to reignite that inferno of excitement all over again. It almost gets the chance every now and again when I dig out an old album to listen to or on the rare occasion the radio plays a decent tune. But then it hears the cell phone song and the flame dims back down to a mere flicker.

I know the past is where all that stuff belongs, my fire would not last long in the world of 50cent, Niki Minaj or Drake but I now know that in 20 years time people full of excitement for todays big artists will feel the same way as I do now. They too will lament the standard of music the kids are listening to. This is how it has worked for all of time and that is one thing that will never change. So fire up the turntable and stick a right old belter on.

Give Me A Break

Most people these days like to travel. Supposedly it has never been easier to see the world. Anyone can log onto their internet and book a flight, hotel and car hire with the click of a couple of buttons. You could, provided you have the funds, book a holiday from your damp dismal bedsit in Scunthorpe on Monday morning and within hours be basking on a beach in Barbados, snapping selfies with your Singapore Sling for your Instagram. It all sounds very jet set.

Before you disappear off to the Caribbean let me point out why I think traveling and in particular air travel, may not be all it is cracked up to be.

I'll spare you the details of all the usual strife caused by the pre holiday shopping, packing and preparations. That stuff is a pain for everyone. We shall begin on the morning of your departure. Flight is at 7am, don't sleep in. At 3am you are awakened from a shallow slumber by the shrieking air raid siren that is your alarm clock. No one in the history of time has ever got a good nights shut-eye before a holiday. Thats just a fact and it's a fitting way to start the potential nightmare that awaits you.

You stumble out of bed, get washed and skip breakfast, that can be taken care of in the purgatory that is the departure lounge. You pack up the car, lock up the house and make your way to the gateway to paradise, or maybe hell. At this point you don't know which way this holiday will go.

Upon your arrival at the airport at least 2 hours before your flight leaves, you are greeted by your new pass time for the foreseeable future...waiting and queuing. Todays modern airports have all sorts innovative schemes and procedures to ease your progress through the departure lounge and invariably they do not work. Convenient bag drop areas and priority boarding all sound great but they have one major flaw, everyone wants to be first, everyone wants to get to the plane quickly and with as little hassle as possible. With passenger levels continuously increasing, airports struggle to cope with the influx of people. So it becomes an ironic twist that the longest queues form exactly where they are supposed to move quickest. At one UK airport I actually witnessed a strange anomaly. A long queue formed at the priority security line and people kept joining it. This perplexed me as the normal peasant line that I was in was all but empty. I just could not fathom it, people had actually paid a few quid extra to get to what is essentially a waiting room quicker, but due to the desire to move quickly they actually ended up standing in line longer.

On that note, with your bags checked you head off to the lottery that is the queue for security. This time you didn't win and have no choice but to join the long winding line that leads to the cattle market that is the security area. You shuffle along with all the other happy souls with your toiletries ready for inspection. The planets have aligned and the universe has decreed that you will now become part of the longest and slowest queue ever known to man. As you move deeper into this jungle you will witness behaviour that verges on the animalistic. Childish temper tantrums, parental anguish, pensioner bewilderment and businessman superiority are just some of the traits you will be exposed to and there will always be an uncontrollable little spawn of Satan covered in his own bogies nearby. He ensures your time spent here will be that much more unbearable.

After considerable anguish you make it to the front of the line. Here, anguish turns to despair. You are an intelligent person, you know the rules, put all your objects into the tray, all liquids are under the 100 ml requirement and sealed in one of those little plastic bags. Watches, belts, phones and keys are all given up to the bored and disinterested security guy who has been telling the same instructions to hundreds of people all day long. Any wonder he is disinterested. He has to stand everyday and watch these happy people tell him that they have nothing in their pockets but lint and that there are absolutely no liquid items whatsoever in their bags. He then looks on as the person lights up all the machines like Christmas trees because they are incapable of following simple instructions. You have spent an eternity queuing because dopy Dave has a belt with a buckle the size of his head that he thought a metal detector wouldn't detect. Bewildered Belinda throws a strop because her bag is being emptied out in front of the world because she thinks the litre bottle of water buried at the bottom of her handbag doesn't count as a liquid. One of the most frustrating things you can ever encounter is when other peoples incompetence holds you up.

Once you have made it through this ordeal and successfully retrieved your belt before suffering an embarrassing trouser related incident, you enter the bright shiny world of the departure prison. With your new found restrictive freedom to roam the duty free shops and restaurants, you take the opportunity to grab some breakfast because by this stage your stomach thinks your throat has been cut. Incidentally, buying anything in an airport departure lounge will cost you the equivalent of a small nations national debt, but as a prisoner you have no choice. The last time I travelled I plumped for a basic sausage on toast with a mug of tea and they helped themselves to 15 quid out of my back pocket.

In an effort to preserve your capital you find a seat in some far off corner and sit on it, waiting and waiting for the big tv screen to instruct you to move to the gate. You end up glued to this screen in fear of missing some sort of nonexistent important update from the Gods of travel. Time now seems to move backwards. Your beard has now grown considerably longer than it was when you embarked on your adventure and your shaving foam and razor are out of reach and being thrown about like a volleyball by a couple of disgruntled baggage handlers.

After an eternity your gate number is revealed and you rush to gather all your kith and kin and begin the trek to the mythical gate.

Eventually you arrive there sweaty, tired and broken. You are greeted with guess what, another queue. A strange thing happens here, people just have to be the first on the plane. Why? It won't suddenly leave, you have booked, paid and have an allocated seat. Whats the rush now?

Once aboard the metal tube you sink into your cramped and suspiciously stained seat. The plane starts to move and the safety announcement is like music to your ears. The thought that you will have to go through this all again in a week or so could not be further from your mind.

Lie back, headphones in and relax, but you are disturbed by a sharp thump and violent shudder. Is there something wrong with the plane? Are we going to crash? No, it's something much worse. Little Satan with the bogies, the monster from the security queue is casually kicking the life out of the back of your seat. Those left behind on the ground look up in confusion as your screams fade off into the blue yonder.

You have paid probably several thousand pounds for the privilege of all this misery. I've read stories about high flying business men and politicians paying similar amounts to have much less torture inflicted on them by dominatrixes in the dungeons of Soho. They should simply go on holidays, at least they wouldn't make the front page of the papers.

Next time I'll pay the outsize baggage charge and check myself into the hold. At least it would be a more relaxing and comfortable journey.

The Emperor's Old Clothes

You probably all know the old story of the Emperor with a penchant for parading about in the buff. You likely had this story told to you as a child and while it probably raised a few giggles in the classroom, the message was serious and would stand you in good stead for the rest of your life. Don't be an ignorant gullible bastard. Maybe I'm simplifying that a little but you get the idea.

Lately I've been pondering my wardrobe or rather the stuff inside it. I do this from time to time but rarely does my pondering turn into action. I stand in front of the collection of garments I have amassed over the years. A range of tatty t-shirts and jeans for everyday use, the two suits for more formal occasions, several shirts of the casual variety and a modest collection of footwear. Trainers, boots, and shoes, two pairs of each in the standard brown, black or white. Also the holiday flip-flops that get an outing once a year if they're lucky. This is my wardrobe. It is not extravagant by any means but it does the job of covering up my unsightly wobbly bits.

As I have gotten older the thought of fashion has started to worry me. Im not concerned with looking fashionable or dressing in a style appropriate for my age. In fact my worry is the exact opposite. You see over the past few years I have started to notice a strange phenomenon amongst those deemed to be of a certain age. I call it the beige creep. The main symptoms of this terrible disease seem to start small. Maybe a beige pair of socks slip into your drawer, then some trousers followed by a jumper and before you know it your whole world is draped in a thick heavy blanket the colour of a hospital hearing aid. Your clothes are beige, your shoes are beige even your car and the way you drive it becomes beige.

You may have noticed it too, it might even have already afflicted you but why and how does this happen? When does the change take place? When do you hang up your trendy jeans and favour a nice comfortable pair of beige easy iron slacks instead?

I have tried to have a serious conversation about this with the other half but she dismisses it as silly nonsense.   The joke will be on her when someday she wakes up and finds an old beige pensioner wandering aimlessly around the house.   I assume there is a female equivalent of this problem but if it is so wide spread and affects all of the population, why are we not warned about it in our early years so we can be on our guard against it?   It should be taught alongside the green cross code and held in similar importance as the stranger danger talk.

This beige creep seems to affect all aspects of your life not just your clothes.   Your car becomes dull and practical, your holidays are bland and your food is chosen based on how easy it is to digest rather than how tasty it is to eat.   Even your furniture starts to resemble that found in an old peoples home or musty antique shop.   Life all becomes a bit Enid Blyton.

Im not saying that I want to dress and act like a 21 year old when I'm 71, that would be ridiculous but I'm certainly not going to allow myself to slip quietly into a beige oblivion.   If you haven't been aware of this problem before now consider yourself warned.   You too are in danger of being drafted into the beige brigade.   That army of people who spend their day drudging along to the shop a 6am to buy a paper then drudge home in their beige loafers to sit in a sensible wingback chair and fall asleep before they've reached the bottom of page 2. This is not the future I want. If I so much as even smell a Werther's Original or catch a glimpse of a beige sock in my sock draw I will relinquish all clothes and parade around like an Emperor. I may be cold and I may get some funny looks but at least the only beige I will be sporting will be my own pale arse.

Meeting In The Crapper

From the second you are born you have only a finite amount of time to live. This time is completely unknown, you may have a mere 10 years, 50 years or maybe 100 years. You simply don't know. One thing you can be sure of is that with each tick of the clock you are edging ever closer to the moment when the light goes out permanently and you slip into the great void that is death. When you are young the problem of time generally doesn't bother you. Summers are long and time seems never-ending, but as you get on in years time seems to accelerate out of control. It becomes ever more important to try and make the most of each second as it slips through your fingers.

There are many things that could be considered a waste of time. I've already made my feelings known on what a waste of time watching reality TV, queuing and health and safety can be. However there is one activity that overshadows all of these and is forced upon millions of people around the world everyday. It is the activity of meetings.

You will undoubtably have had to take part in some form of meeting and I bet you found it to be an utter waste of time, unless you were one of the organisers of it. Then you probably thought it was a great success and time well spent.

I spent some time in a meeting lately and the break down went something like this.

10 minutes waiting for everyone to arrive and get settled.

5 minutes waiting for some people who had the good sense not to show up.

5 minutes apologising for those people who couldn't make it because they were engaged in another meeting or who were hiding in the stationery cupboard.

15 minutes recapping the last tedious meeting.

30 minutes of hot air, ass kissing and exchanging phrases like, blue sky thinking, managing customer expectations, running things up flag poles and lots of touching base. Whatever that means.

And finally 10 minutes congratulating each other on how well the free form exchange of ideas apparently went.

At the 15 minute mark I was genuinely considering drowning myself in the glass of tepid complementary water in front of me. I've even been to meetings where the sole purpose was to discuss and organise another meeting. In these corporate get togethers, corporate manslaughter becomes a real possibility.

It's not just the fact that the majority of meetings are unproductive and mind numbingly, spirit crushingly boring. The entire culture and language used is frustratingly annoying and prattish. The idea of the boring junior manager in his Topman suit talking about the benefits of hot desking and thinking outside of his box is enough to drive me to the nuthouse. I sit there thinking about how he would look with his Parker pen jammed in his ear and his business mans Blackberry shoved up his business end. It reminds me of the old image of the jumped up junior manager striding confidently through the office with his shiny faux leather briefcase with nothing more than his lunch inside it. The modern equivalent is the Samsung tablet with nothing more than Angry Birds or Candy Crush inside.

A long time ago in a previous life I worked for a well known supermarket chain where every little apparently helped. As a so-called team leader I was required to attend a daily morning meeting. All the great and the good attended to discuss the issues of the day. I used to sit there amazed at how engrossed they seemed to be when discussing exciting topics such as this weeks baked bean bonanza. They could drag out the most inane and boring subject for an hour or more when in reality they could have just spend five minutes fixing whatever the problem was without wasting anyone else's time. It was all just empty talk to make them seem important. They jostled for recognition in a vain attempt to claw their way up another rung on the corporate ladder. My personal breaking point was after the 3rd meeting which turned out to be about the exciting topic of broccoli. With each minute that passed a little piece of me withered and died. The final blow came when the enthusiastic trainee produce manager produced an A6 laminated card listing all his broccoli based issues in handy bullet point form. It even had a small picture of a broccoli just incase you weren't entirely familiar with the little green super vegetable.

At this point in life I was in my early twenties. I had my whole life ahead of me but not if this nonsense continued. I politely excused myself from the meeting, headed straight to the home furnishing department, grabbed a pillow, buried my head deep into the polyester duck down and screamed like I was being murdered. Obviously a new job was needed, preferably one that didn't involve meetings. Unfortunately these don't seem to exist, even the unemployed have to have meetings to discuss their employability. I fear that even a community of hermits living on the most isolated peaks known to man meet regularly to discuss pressing hermit issues.

A hasty research mission revealed a recent article published on a site with the highly imaginative name, RealBusiness.co.uk. It shows just how widespread the problem is. They revealed that the average UK worker is dragged along to 3.7 meetings per week. They claim they spend 1 hour 9 minutes preparing for the meeting and spend 1 hour 22 minutes locked in a room against their will listening to bullshit. They cite that over a 40 year career an average middle manager will spend 17,470 hours preparing and attending meetings. This equates to almost 2 full years of an average persons entire life. Thats huge when compared to the fact that the same average person spends just 92 days of their life sitting on the bog.

I have given this problem much thought and the only time saving conclusion that I can think of is to combine these two tedious activities. Swap out the corporate office chairs for a porcelain pot. If nothing else being fired by Lord Sugar would be that much more amusing if he was perched on the shitter at the time.

57 Channels & Nothing On

If there are any Bruce Springsteen fans reading this you will probably know his 1992 song of the same name. It certainly wasn't one of his biggest or well known hits but its lyrics pop into my head almost every time I switch on the electric picture box. Today in the UK TV comes in a mind boggling variety of packages and options, from the basic Freeview option to the million channel satellite and cable options and everything else in between. This is a long way away from the first flickering broadcasts John Logie Baird created in 1926. Even when I was growing up I was spoilt with the massive choice of 4 channels.

As I flick through my electronic TV guide I can't help but ponder if television has actually improved since it was first invented. Of course the technology has improved immensely over the last 70 years or so. Picture quality is miles better now compared to even a few years ago, screen sizes are huge, special effects are mind boggling and moving a television set is no longer considered a strongman event, but has the actual content improved?

Presently on my tv only 5 channels of the several hundred or so available are broadcasting brand new programmes and two of them are sporting fixtures. All the rest are repeats of programmes that seem to be shown on some sort of long running continuous loop. Like the scene from Crocodile Dundee when he arrives at his hotel in New York and sees the TV set in his room. He explains that he has seen tv before and switches it on only to be greeted by an image of the I Love Lucy show which aired in the 1960s. He concludes that yes that was what he saw last time he saw tv and promptly switches it off again. This tongue in cheek scene was filmed in the 1980s and I can't see that things have improved any.

I remember a time when if there was a programme you wanted to watch you had to set time aside to watch it, organise your schedule around it and hope no one interrupted your viewing with a phone call or some such inconvenience. You even had to plan your toilet breaks to coincide with the commercial breaks. Your only option of later viewing was to record the show onto a jittery old VHS tape. Now you can pause, rewind, stream or catch up on TV anytime and anywhere but again I think why? I can find very little I actually want to watch today or that I haven't seen before so the option of watching it at my convenience appears largely irrelevant.

I think this on demand screen culture is harming people more than any other technological advance today. People live out their entire lives staring into screens without ever really taking the time to look around at the beauty of their own surroundings. Yes, you can see the great wall of China in full HD, experience the beaches of Tahiti in Ultra HD and see the pyramids in 4k. This is all marvellous, but you haven't seen a real live squirrel in your local forest or a fish in a nearby stream. You can recite the names of the entire cast of Eastenders but you don't know the names of your next door neighbours.

It seems to me that as the technological world expands our own real life world shrinks. Our lives become more insular as we sit there in a daze aimlessly watching other peoples experiences on screen while ignoring the need to create experiences and adventures of our own.

That can't be good for anyone. Sometimes I yearn for the return of the good old days with only four channels, a small screen and a big wide world to explore.

The Terminators Kettle

A friend of mine had an uninvited guest last Christmas. She invaded his home on Christmas Day, but the police were not interested, nor was Interpol or the NCA, even the Salvation Army didn't care and christmas is their big time.

No, this uninvited guest was welcomed by all in the household except my mate Jim. He was deeply suspicious of his new house guest and could tell sinister intentions were afoot.

This insignificant little intrusion had a name, it was called Alexa or Dot or Echo or something. She sat there on the kitchen counter, listening, gleaning information about Jim and his family and storing it for future use. The rest of the family believed this was incredibly useful, they only had to ask her to do something and it was done. "Alexa, Dim the lights" and darkness fell across the room. "Alexa, play my playlist" and your favourite music drifts across the left over turkey and cold brussel sprouts. Jim was thinking about calling in an exorcist to rid his house of this supernatural being. He had seen 2001 A Space Odyssey and he was increasingly nervous of handing over control of his life to any sort of artificial intelligence. He doesn't trust this little box thats sits listening to every word, waiting for the opportunity to take control of the house and his life.

I have to say I side with Jim on this, not because I'm paranoid or because Alexa might just be the forerunner to the terminator. My view, and you are probably not going to be surprised by this, is that this sort of technology seems completely unnecessary to me. It seems to have been born out of laziness rather than actual need. If I want my lights dimmed I'll do it myself using my arms and legs thank you very much.

This whole thing seems to have started years ago, pre 2000 when everything had to either have an "e" before its name or a .com after it. Then came Apple who launched its "i" range. Then everything had to have an "i" in its name. Stick the letter "i" in front of anything and it instantly becomes cool. I think at one point you could have called a dog poo an iTurd and someone would have bought it for hundreds of pounds. The "i" thing seems to be passing now but it has been replaced by the "Smart" prefix. As far as I can tell this just means it connects to the Interweb.

You have smart watches, smart TVs , smart fridges and even smart lightbulbs. Some bloke even tried to sell me a smart kettle the other day. He claimed you could boil your kettle from the comfort of your own sofa. I could set the desired temperature using an app on my iphone and the kettle would do the rest. You can even ask Alexa and she will do it for you. I pointed out that once the kettle had in fact boiled I would still have to make the arduous journey into the kitchen, physically remove the 98.7 degree water from the device and actually make whatever hot beverage I wanted. My phone was not capable of performing this task nor is it capable of actually putting water into the blasted thing to start with. He didn't seem to understand where I was coming from and kept insisting that it was the best thing since knife met bread. I argued that sliced bread actually was a break through because it really did save time, his kettle device was merely a gimmick. He began to sense my hostility towards him and his idiotic contraption and tried to usher me away so he could pounce on some other unsuspecting shopper but I wasn't finished yet.

"How much is this kettle anyway?" I asked. "£99.99" he exclaimed. I was speechless, well almost. He must have seen the look of shock and disgust on my face and tried to mount a defence by explaining that the app was completely free, it came with a 60 day money back guarantee and free 24 hour customer supporter or some such twaddle.

100 quid for a kettle, nonsense. I could hire someone to come round every morning and make me a cup of tea from my old kettle and i'd still have change in my pocket. I began to look around to see if I could spot a hidden camera, there was no way this could be a genuine sales pitch.

"Does it boil water any quicker than the kettle I've already got? Does it fill itself up when empty? Will it deliver a ready made cup of tea with a custard cream on the side to my sofa?" I asked in all seriousness.

His defence was valiant but ultimately piss poor. He crumbled and his face turned the colour of an overly ripe tomato. "No" came his reply. "So what idiot would want to spend £100 on such a fatuous piece of kit?" I asked. The young man said nothing, he simply reached below his pop up counter and took out a sign that said, "Back in 15 minutes." He placed it on the counter and walked away with a trail of steam coming from his ears. I don't think my line of questioning was particularly harsh or unreasonable but as I had successfully ruined his day I decided my work there was done and headed home for a cuppa.

Occasionally when I'm enjoying a cup of warm brown I think about the red faced man and his funny kettle and wonder whatever happened to him. Ive certainly never seen him in that shop again. I like to think that our little interaction led him to change his whole way of life. Perhaps he has shunned his 5G kettles and his app loaded lifestyle and is living a simpler and happier life in some far away tropical paradise. Or maybe he is still pushing his silly gimmicks in another nondescript department store on a grey concrete retail park on a drizzle filled Saturday afternoon.

What about my mate Jim you ask. What became of him? Jim's family kept their new cyber friend. She is one of the family now, they even bought a new kettle for her to use. Jim now lives in his garden shed with his old kettle but at least he's happy.

Manners, What Manners?

When I was growing up good manners were drilled into you from before you could gargle your milk formula. You dared not speak to an elder unless spoken to first. You had respect and fear for those in authority and you knew how and when to say please and thank you. At the very least you knew how to hold a knife and fork properly. I've seen young ones in restaurants holding their fork like some sort of primitive spear, as if their piece of cow on a plate wasn't quite dead yet and was just lying behind the potatoes waiting for an opportunity to make a dash for freedom. Not only that, the kids of today seem incapable of just sitting quietly at the table and eating their dinner while the grown ups talk. Instead they run around the table hollering and roaring like they are performing some sort of native tribal dance to thank the god of vegetables for providing sustenance. I like to see families out enjoying themselves and spending time together. However when the parents are cowering under the table while their little cherubs run riot terrorising the waiting staff and offending the other diners, I can't help but think what did I do to deserve this torture and why are you inflicting your ill-mannered offspring on me?

I know my next point might be somewhat controversial but hear me out. I was always told that it was right and proper to hold a door open for those coming behind you. If that person happened to be a lady, you stood back, held the door for them and allowed them to go first. I'm sure there are some sections of society that will claim this is an out dated practice maybe even perceived as sexist or even misogynistic. Conversely the same people would probably berate me if I barged on ahead letting the door slam shut in the surprised woman's face. It's the social conundrum of the times we live in but I think I'll stick to the old ways and here's why.

Manners are the cornerstone of society, without them we become akin to the dumb uncivilised beasts in the field. At school when a teacher entered the room the sound of chairs scraping along the hard floor was deafening as the entire class sprang to their feet. Mouths shut you stood there until you had permission to retake your seat. This was what was expected, even my mate

Willie was expected to spring to attention and he only had one leg. He used to stand there wobbling about, sweat breaking on his brow. On at least one occasion he toppled over causing an outburst of gasps followed by uncontrollable laughter. Naturally the teacher saw this as a deliberate act of anarchy and issued poor Willie with a detention. He protested his innocence of course but unfortunately he hadn't a leg to stand on. (Sorry). Teachers in my day were infallible, most authority figures in those days were. No doubt some abused their power so maybe its a good thing that things aren't just as strict as this anymore. I fear however that things have gone too far the other way. Teachers are in fear of their little angels now and woe betide they tell a parent their little angels behaviour is anything less than exemplary.

Even the police command little or no respect from todays youth. They are seen as a target for abuse and ridicule. In my day if you were caught misbehaving by an officer of the law he would hit you a clip round the ear and drag you home and your parents would apologise for you being an inconvenience, clip you round your remaining good ear and thank PC Plod for alerting them to your delinquency. Now PC Plod would get a severe reprimand from his superiors and the little bastard would continued unencumbered down the road of criminality.

I came into contact with one of these cretins lately and I think the whole situation could have been avoided if his parents had instilled in him a bit of respect during his formative years.

It was a dull Wednesday evening and I was strolling along the short dimly lit pathway that led from the local shop to my house. Out of the shadows stepped a hooded tracksuit clad urchin. His face was stubbly and the smell of cheap drink hung on his breath. He demanded my phone and the 89 pence in assorted change that I had in my pocket. He made it clear great injury would be caused if I didn't immediately comply with his instructions. I could see in his franticly darting eyes that he meant business. I froze, what should I do? All sorts of thoughts raced through my mind. After what seemed like an eternity and 2 black eyes, a broken arm and 3 broken fingers later the constabulary arrived and I assume took the good for nothing degenerate to hospital for treatment. I continued on my stroll home content in the knowledge that maybe I had succeeded in this mans life where others had previously failed him. On the other hand now he's not able to hold his knife and fork properly even if he did know how.

Stop The World I Want To Get Off

Since the beginning of time the human mind has pondered the meaning of life, the reason for our existence and why the world is the way it is. This is completely normal, it is the sign of a healthy inquisitive mind and vital for human progress and survival. It's why we are no longer confined to sitting in a cave drawing crude pictures on the wall and conversing in a series of grunts.

Aristotle the Greek philosopher has been credited as being one of the greatest thinkers of all time. His is just one name in a cast of thousands that has had a hand in formulating our modern knowledge on topics such as science, physics, the human mind and the space-time continuum. It would be amazing if the likes of Plato, Confucius and Machiavelli or even Darwin could come back today and see how much we had developed and how accurate or indeed inaccurate their theories actually were. Then again they may despair at some of the theories circulating today.

Of course history has had its fair share of bonkers ideas over the years. The middle ages were rife for crackpot ideas. Blood letting, demonic possession, witch burning and divine celestial punishments had all been credible and widely held beliefs of the time which thankfully have now been largely dispelled through modern scientific thinking. At one time it was considered heresy to claim that the earth was not at the centre of the universe or that it was indeed anything other than flat in dimension. At best you could be imprisoned for your decadent beliefs, at worst it could cost you your life. Galileo fell foul of this after adopting Copernicus' views on the solar system and was imprisoned for life after a particularly strict and entirely one sided inquisition. Luckily we now have space travel, powerful telescopes, video and photographic evidence to convince the average peasant how things actually work. After all they say seeing is believing.

Even with all the scientific capabilities and evidence at our disposal today there are still certain sections of the population that refuse to move out of the dark ages and continue to observe the world around them through the wrong end of the binoculars.

There are those who believe that the governments of the world are using commercial planes to chemically control the population. Apparently 17% of the people believe this to be true. Some believe that JFK's assassination was shrouded in a cover up of some kind. Others believe Hitler survived the war and fled to Antarctica. A theory exists that a new world order is in control of the entire planet and some say that this new order lives in a hidden underground city underneath Denver Airport. Maybe the illuminati are in charge or maybe it's the Freemasons or 5G who knows. Maybe it's really Elvis shaking things up. I've even heard a rumour that Queen Liz herself keeps a flock of lizard people in her garden.

It seems that no matter what the topic or event there is a fairly deranged section of society that insists on living in an alternative reality. Some of these people are well known, somewhat respected and very well educated. Rumours have circulated for years that Tom Cruise believes a big space lizard called Xenu rules the world. Utter bonkers.

While all these theories are undoubtably wacky and too much research into these things could lead you down an inescapable rabbit hole, there is one theory that really does irritate me in its unrivalled stupidity. That is the Flat Earthers. This group of misinformed twits rigorously believe that the earth is flat. Despite all the evidence presented to dispute this they cannot comprehend that the earth is in fact round, how could it be? People in Australia would be upside down and would simply fall off into oblivion. I've mentioned my encounters with one of these flat earthers in a previous chapter and he too displayed the response most conspiracy theorists do when presented with a rational, evidenced based argument. Rather than say, "My god you're right, I've wasted my life, I've been duped, thank you for enlightening me" they say "Ahh I see they've got to you too, your mind is closed to whats really happening" How do you even begin to argue with this mentality?

Perhaps Aristotle, Plato, Hitler, Elvis and a big lizard are all living on a remote island somewhere in the South Pacific, shrouded behind a cloak of smoke and mirrors, secretly pulling the levers that control all of human activity.

My solution would be to round up all these confused individuals and move them secretly to a deserted island. Secret cameras could then record their daily activities and we could watch them formulate hair-brain theories as to what the hell happened and how they got there. Thats one reality tv show I might actually watch. In any case even if a collection of business men with a rolled up trouser leg and a funny handshake are in cahoots with space lizards to control what you have for dinner, what exactly are you going to do about it?

Intermission

I realise that this book is probably not long enough to warrant an intermission but the aim of this page is not for you to rest your weary eyes. Rather it is to ensure you take vital steps now to guarantee you get to finish reading it in peace and quiet.

Undoubtedly you have not told your other half that you are sitting with your feet up reading a book. You have probably led them to believe you are finally looking at that leaky radiator that they have been nagging you to fix for the last six months.

As you have been missing for the last hour or so you are in danger of being remembered and that will prompt a routine check by the guard. To avoid suspicion you should now head to the kitchen and update the missus on your progress.

Inform her that after an extensive examination you are confident that you can rectify the problem. Explain that you are now going to replace the quarter inch split pressure valve nut on the inlet receiver pipe. This will not only sound like you know what you are doing but also so incredibly boring that it will dissuade her from getting involved.

To finish the deception offer to make a cup of tea. This will register in her subconscious the fact that all manual labour must be carried out with a strong cuppa in a chipped mug. With a bit of luck she might even make it for you.

Fetch a spanner from the tool shed to complete the illusion, collect your tea and head back to the safety of these pages confident that you have avoided being rumbled by the warden.

For extra safety you could employ the services of one of the more trusted sprogs in the household to keep watch and warn of approaching patrols with the well established bird whistle as used by POWs while in the stalag.

Just don't forget to take 5 minutes at the end of the book to actually fix the leaky radiator or you'll end up in the cooler. Again.

I'm Not A Fanatic

There are a few things I am enthusiastic and passionate about. Music, comedy, cars and astronomy will all pluck up my interest. Some people revel in stamp collecting, some dress up in brightly coloured anoraks and get excited looking at trains. Some enjoy dressing up in combat fatigues and run about a muddy field pretending to be Field Marshal Rommel and some people are even interested in gardening. Whatever your interest is, providing its not cycling based, I say knock yourself out, good luck to you.

One thing I cannot understand is the need for millions of people to become completely wrapped up in the activity of sport. I can understand those who take part in a particular activity as their main occupation being infatuated with whatever their passion is. Even an accountant can be passionate about accounting, in fact you'd have to be to spend your working life as an accountant. An accounting convention probably sounds like most peoples idea of a slow painful death but to a professional number cruncher it would be a hotbed of maths and tax legislation.   Exciting stuff.

I have never been that interested in sport. I just wasn't bothered by it.   I didn't care how fast someone I didn't know could run 100 meters or how many times a multi-millionaire could kick a pigs bladder into a net in 90 minutes. It was of no consequence to me at all.   I enjoyed some sports immensely when I was younger, I played golf and enjoyed swimming. I spent many hours under water looking for lost golf balls, but the idea of spending my free time watching someone else doing this stuff was completely foreign to me. Anyway most sports involve dressing up in some sort of silly clothing that insists on telling me to just do it.

All day everyday I listen to people debate every football, rugby, tennis, cricket and golf game that has taken place since the day before. They spend hours having heated debates about what this player should have done or what that manager should do next.   To hear them you would be forgiven for thinking that they actually had some say in the running of whatever club they are talking about.   That a manager who is paid millions every year to make these vital decisions is sitting eagerly by his phone waiting for Dave in accounting to impart his valuable insights. I often wonder if people are genuinely interested in what they are talking about or are they just using it as small talk to avoid one of those socially awkward silences.

Hours and hours are lost everyday in these heated debates which in reality have no bearing or benefit to those involved. The same thing happens at all televised sporting events. A half hour introduction and build up. A running commentary and action replays throughout the match and then and eternity of post match analysis. It drives me nuts. I can watch an interesting, fast paced film for 90 minutes and I don't need a half hour introduction to it, action replays or post film analysis about what I've just seen. I might mention it to a friend the next day in passing, maybe even recall a particularly good scene. We don't sit around for hours discussing how the director could have done this or that differently or how the lighting guy made a balls of the atmospheric romance scene. It's just enjoyed for what it is, entertainment.

Imagine if all the energy that people around the world put into sporting debates was redeployed into more useful activities. Problems like world hunger, poverty, climate change and religious bigotry could all be solved. It's possible that there would be a real danger world peace could break out.

I really don't believe that people will stop agonising over their inconsequential sporting events, so that means I have to come up with a way of dealing with these incredulous individuals on a daily basis. You could say, "I'm not really into sport" but that will only encourage looks of disgust and disbelief. I've found that the average person is very suspicious of someone who doesn't like sport. Maybe thats the answer, give them something to be suspicious about.

Whenever someone attempts to entangle you in a sport related conversation start to develop a twitch of some sort, nothing major to start with just enough to be noticeable. After a while start shouting out random sporting names or objects along with your twitch. This will undoubtably lead to many questions and you can take it as far as you want to. Start scribbling over the faces of sports people in the newspaper and then set fire to the entire sports section. Try dropping little snippets about your psychiatrists sessions into the conversation, the world is your oyster. Eventually people will stop talking to you and if you're lucky they may even avoid you all together. The downside is that if you push it too far they will think you are actually mad and have you committed to some sort of secure unit, but if you are truly dedicated it's a risk worth taking.

Alternatively you could simply fart. Thats usually a very effective conversation stopper.

What's The Point?

I hope you have enjoyed the book so far, hopefully my musings have been somewhat lighthearted, interesting and humorous. If not then I applaud your stubbornness for wanting to finish what you've started. That is a great trait for the professional grump to have. Please continue...

Before I dive head first into the quagmire that is our country, I feel an apology may be in order. This chapter may get a bit personal, to me that is, maybe more personal than I would really like but anyway here goes.

Religious persecution and sectarian violence has plagued many countries and societies over the years, my little corner of the world is no different. I grew up knowing nothing else. Violence had been common place here for generations, long before I ever arrived. My impact and participation in the whole sordid affair is at most irrelevant but its impact on me is quite the opposite.

My upbringing was no different to anyone else living here, life was what it was, we played with the same toys as the rest of the world, we ate the same foods as the rest of the world and we did all the same things as the rest of the world, however it was all done under a cloud of something very sinister. A war that had bubbled on for hundreds of years. This meant that your religion dictated where you lived, what school you went to, who your friends were, what sports you played, who you married and even what pubs you drank in. The religious divide permeated almost every aspect of life here.

The trouble came in waves but flared up significantly in the sixties and continued right the way through my childhood. The army and police patrolled the streets in large groups, they crouched hidden in hedges and around corners, military checkpoints were routine if not expected. Helicopters flew overhead and occasionally the loud bang of a bomb exploding, followed by the inevitable shuddering of windows, rocked my hometown. Men with woolly faces, camouflage jackets and guns controlled their respective areas and emerged into each other's turf to attack and maim their perceived enemies.

My country had rules that at the time I thought completely normal. Large barriers closed off all vehicle access to the town centre after business hours to prevent car bombs being detonated overnight. During the day one person had to be left in the car when it was parked in the town, any unattended vehicle risked being blasted to smithereens just in case it was packed with explosives. You couldn't travel more than a mile or two by car without being stopped by the authorities, asked for ID and questioned as to where you might be heading to. Many times I had to take the long way home from school because some reckless and cowardly bastard had left a carload of explosives right along the way I would usually have walked and the army was now trying to make it safe by blowing it up in something called a controlled explosion.

The daily news was different too. Each morning before school I would watch our stern newsreader tell us that someone be they civilian, army, police or terrorist had been shot the night before, a mortar attack had been thwarted somewhere or a bomb had been found under someone's car. Occasionally they informed us which town no longer existed today as it did yesterday. Bomb damage sales really were a thing here.

Before my 16th birthday my hometown had been blown up three times and numerous other attempts had been foiled. This was normal for most people right across the country. Thousands of lives were lost during the years of conflict here and countless others irreparably damaged. At times rumours of ceasefires circulated and talks took place but the hope this brought was often blown to pieces. 1996 saw a huge blast rip through London's Docklands killing 2 people. This marked the end of a 17 month IRA ceasefire and was followed up by a bigger blast in Manchester a few months later. This one was the biggest bomb detonated in England since world war 2. These are just two examples when trouble spilled over to the mainland but there were many others.

It wasn't until a so called peace broke out in the spring of 1998 that things began to change or rather that was the idea. In the summer of that same year the worst atrocity of the conflict happened when a bomb ripped through a small provincial town killing 31 people including two unborn twins and injuring hundreds more.

Eventually peace took a shaky and fragile hold and things began to slowly change. New buildings sprang up, tourists began to arrive and the country began to develop. The news began to feature stories that didn't involve bombings and shootings. It was a slow process but many people outside of here really knew very little about our strange little country and its history.

I went on holiday to Tenerife in the early 2000s and as usual found myself chatting to an English person. They lived not more than 200 miles across a small channel of water from where I did. Undoubtably perplexed by my accent they asked me where I was from. When I told them, I was somewhat taken aback by their response. They looked at me with a puzzled look and asked quite seriously, "Whats it like there? Do you have electricity and TV and stuff? At first I thought they were taking the micky out of the Irish bloke, but looking back I can see why they must have thought this. They only knew my country by the grainy news reports and documentaries that made it to their regional tv channels and quaint Irish postcards of thatched cottages and rugged country types with no teeth harvesting turf. They were as far removed from us as we were from the plight of famine in Ethiopia.

In the years since the millennium our little country has begun to move on but often the movement is slow and sometimes backwards. There are still those that seem determined to live in the past, they focus on the same old problems and spout the same old rhetoric. There are still some small scale bombings and shootings and tensions between communities are strained at times but we have had a taste of peace and prosperity and it tastes so much sweeter than the bitter past. Thats why when I see people treat the opportunity we have with such reckless disregard and seem willing to throw away all that has been achieved on a whim, it makes my blood boil.

When I switch on my local news now I am greeted by the sight of politicians sniping at each other like school children, stories about the past and legacy issues that can never be solved amicably dominate the airwaves. Our country is facing forward but our politicians are still facing backwards. With each day that passes we seem to slide ever closer to the past . That bitter taste returns to the back of your throat from deep down in your stomach as you watch the old tensions bubble beneath the veneer of peace in a place that on the surface is desperately trying to look normal.

More often than not I refuse to watch the news. It depresses me and makes me want to give up on this place I call home. I want to move to a new country far away from the bombs, bullets and problems of the past. I sometimes think what life would have been like if I was born somewhere else. Somewhere that the problems of my country were irrelevant and unknown, Jamaica, France, Spain, America or maybe even Wales, wherever, it doesn't matter, but then I think the people there have problems too albeit different ones. I'd simply be swapping one set of problems for another that are equally engulfing and suffocating to the communities that live there. I realise that my home is here, as troubled, backward, frustrating and embarrassing as it is. I belong in Northern Ireland.

King Tut's Trots

Egypt is a magical and mystical country. During a three thousand year period starting from about 3100BC one of the greatest civilisations that ever existed thrived in an arid desert in North Africa. Fuelled by the life giving River Nile, a succession of Pharaohs with their legions of hardworking subjects and slaves carved the most wonderful temples, pyramids and monuments that thousands of years later still evoke a feeling of awe and utter wonderment.

When you think of Egypt visions of sun drenched pyramids float into your head. Great leaders adorned with beautiful jewels and gold trinkets ride around on top of chariots and mystical cursed tombs hiding long held secrets and treasures are around every corner.

It is this image that draws thousands of visitors to this hot arid place every year. I've been there and I loved it, however my image of this magical place has been somewhat tainted.

We arrived at sunset in mid July and as I stepped off the plane I was greeted by a wall of heat that seemed to emanate straight from the sun god Ra himself. The smell of the hot desert surrounded us and you could see the last heat of the day hover and shimmer between the dark tarmac of the runway and the deep orange sky. By the time we left the airport and got on the coach the sun had completely vanished and an inky darkness fell over the sand and rocks. Only the pale sliver of silver light from the moon gave any clue to the fact that there was a vast hidden landscape beyond the dim headlights of the bus.

As we walked through the entrance of our hotel we were greeted by the welcoming coolness of the air conditioning and staff wearing the whitest pressed uniforms I've ever seen. A small buggy transferred us to our room and all manner of food was adorned upon us as we looked out over the calm blue water of our pool. It was truly magical.

The next morning we were calmly woken from our slumber by the sun god gently streaming his pale yellow rays though our white curtains.

Over the next few days we indulged in everything the Egyptians had to offer. It was on day three while sitting beside the pool that I began to sense that something just wasn't quite right. It happened quickly and very unexpectedly. A disturbing rumble rippled around me. Was it a far off thunderstorm on the horizon? Maybe some sort of catastrophic building collapse from the construction site across the street? A quick glance revealed that the sky continued to be beautifully clear and the surrounding buildings stood firm. The distant rumble was closer than I first thought. It originated from my stomach. Could it be hunger? No, I hadn't long finished breakfast. The more astute amongst you will have realised where this is heading. The rumbling became more frequent, more intense, then came the inevitable cramping. It was time to move. I made it without a second to spare. Diarrhoea of truly biblical proportions followed. The noises emanating from that wash cubicle would have woken a Pharaoh and probably haven't been heard by human ears since Moses parted the Red Sea. I was left crippled and exhausted, a shadow of my former self. After what seemed like hours I dragged my worthless husk of a body to the bed and died.

When I woke it was dark, several hours must have passed since my episode. The room was cool but a bead of sweat rolled from my forehead. I lay there contemplating what had happened, was it some sort of assassination attempt? Was I the victim of a cruel prank? Had I been afflicted by some remnant of Egypts great biblical plagues or had I transgressed some ancient being and was now suffering his curse? I gathered my thoughts and decided to try and get up. A note was stuck to the dresser. It read "Gone to dinner, water in the fridge." In our family a man can be left behind. I gathered what little strength I had and shuffled my way to the dinning room like some sort of geriatric mummy wrapped in bog roll. Pale and broken I made it to the table, slumped in a chair and received that look that only a woman can give. It's the one that encompasses pity, anger, disappointment and embarrassment all at once. I didn't think it wise to eat so I avoided the buffet cart and just sipped gingerly at a glass of water. I'd paid good money for this holiday, stood through airport security and put up with the little bastard kicking the back of my seat for 2500 miles. I was damned if I was going to let an inconvenient little microbe ruin it. After 20 minutes or so I thought I felt slightly better. I was on the mend, I had won. Oh how foolish I was.

As I rose from the table and pushed my chair back I heard a familiar rumble. I froze. A cold sweat broke on my back. Planted to the spot I weighted up my options. I decided a brisk shuffle to the nearest bathroom was my best option. It was the longest journey of my life. There is nothing funnier or more pathetic than watching someone try and walk as quickly as possible with clenched cheeks, trying to keep their feet no more than 3 inches in front of each other and all the while attempting to look relaxed and normal. I've laughed hysterically at this sort of thing when it happens to other people, now it was my turn to be the butt of the joke.

I suffered through the night making regular trips to the throne room every 30 minutes like clockwork.   Next morning it was clear that something had to be done. As Moses was not around to consult on this plague I decided to try the chemists next to the hotel. The pharmacists shop was small but crammed from floor to ceiling with shelves full of bottles, potions and pills, some even had cobwebs on them. I thought I had stumbled into an Indiana Jones movie and was expecting to find some old wizard of the dunes hidden behind a stack of old scrolls. Instead I was greeted by young man with an Adidas t-shirt and an i-pod. It became apparent that he spoke no English so I reverted to the internationally understood sign language for the squirts. He nodded knowingly and handed me two packets of tablets, one red, one green. He explained, using his watch face, that I was to take a red one every 6 hours and a green one every other hour. I think. I didn't care, I would have happily swallowed both packets in one go if it shored up the dam and held back the relentless brown flow. I have a strong suspicion that shop only ever sold medication for my particular ailment. I threw down the deficit of a small country in used monopoly money and headed briskly but carefully for the door.

By the next day I was feeling better but I was still suspicious of quick moments and unexpected shocks. Then the rumours started. In all at least 10 other people had succumbed to this terrible plague. Apparently it was traced to dodgy chicken from the faux American diner inside the resort. I had seen on the news that tensions were high in the Middle East but I never expected a biological attack on American soil like this.

I have never been back to Egypt since. Not because I'm afraid of getting the King Tut trots again but rather because of the unsettling news I saw when I got home.

Egyptian archaeologists had found a 2000 year old sarcophagus at the start of July. All sorts of rumours circulated, some said it contained the remains of Alexander the Great, Cleopatra or maybe one of the Ramses. Others had more sinister beliefs and talk of a world ending curse being released if the ancient coffin was opened began to spread. Ignoring these fears it was opened and inside 3 skeletal remains were found submerged in the most horrendous ancient raw sewage ever smelt. Im not a superstitious man but its a bit of coincidence that this thing lay buried for 2000 years and the very day it was opened I was struck down with the Tutankhamen trots.

Curses and superstitions aside, I reckon if I had stayed there any longer they would have found me in 2000 years time cocooned in excrement and encased in a tomb that looked suspiciously like a hotel bathroom.

My advice if this happens to you is not to be bitter, don't blame the hotel staff or chefs for their incompetence. Instead be content in the fact that you have left behind a foul smelling ticking time bomb in a country who's plumbing system can't handle even the thinnest of 1 ply toilet paper and some poor bugger is going to have to don a rubber glove and deal with it long after you've gone.

Sweets and Pig Bladders

You probably expect to find in a book like this lots of talk about how monstrous, feckless and useless the young are, and you'd be right. However the old do deserve their share of criticism too. They ramble on incoherently about the good old days, their driving is also incoherent and they move slower than continental drift.

All this aside, I would like to make it abundantly clear that I value old people and their contribution to society. I've always loved listening to the stories told by my elders. I used to love when my Grandfather and his brothers got together and regaled me with memories and tales of their days growing up. Like Uncle Albert most of these stories began with the phrase "During the war". I sat in awe listening to the mischief they caused, the pranks they played and the adventures they had. It was some of the best times of my life and now that they have all passed away I regret not asking to hear more.

One of the best story tellers turned out to be my primary school headmaster Mr Wilson. He was a towering figure with snow white hair and a stern demeanour. This was a man who commanded respect and he didn't let you forget it. He ran that school like a borstal. I was about 10 years old and was in my 6th year at the school when, much to everyone's surprise he let his guard down.

Our usual teacher was away for two days on a training course or some such thing. Looking back he had probably been sent to some sort of therapy to confront his anger issues. This was a man who once broke a school desk in half with a hockey stick because he didn't have the full attention of the shocked miscreant who happened to be sitting behind it at the time.

At 9'o'clock in the morning the towering figure stood at the front of the class and took the roll call. There wasn't a sound apart from the quick barks of "here sir" as we each replied to the sound of our names being called out in a smooth monotone voice. Even at our young age we all knew this was going to be a long few days. Our well meaning but angry teacher had prepared a stack of work for us to do in his absence. First up was a maths worksheet. I remember it well. Question 2 was about weighing out sweets in a sweet shop. I don't know if it was the picture of the old fashioned scales that weighed heavy on the old mans mind or if he was just as bored as we were by the first question. He gently set the worksheet on the desk, took off his glasses and said, "you know I grew up in a house above a sweetshop." He must have sensed that all our attentions had immediately been caught in his net. He went on to tell us exactly where this shop was, we all knew it well. He talked about playing football in the street with pigs bladders filled with air, the blitz, rationing, spitfires, his late parents and angry germans with moustaches. All the things that made this towering teacher who he was today.

We expected this to end at break time and the tedious maths to resume but it didn't, he simply picked up where he left off and carried on down another memory lane, the entire class following his every step. The same happened after lunch and then eventually the bell rang indicating that it was time to go home. He picked up his glasses and said with some emotion "thats enough for today." Truth be told I would gladly have sat on for hours longer listening to his stories. Much like reading a good book, my mind was transported back in time as it compiled a film of this mans past. It was like I was there observing the whole thing like a fly on the wall.

The next day, roll call was taken again. He lifted the maths worksheet from the desk where he had left it the day before. He smiled and set it back down, "Where did we finish off yesterday?" he asked. His face was different from usual, more relaxed and friendly. He continued his trip through his childhood and the whole class sank into listening mode, or at least I thought they did. Turns out some of the arseholes in the class didn't appreciate his stories and mocked his life as being old fashioned and boring. Apparently they felt this mans long and interesting life was not as important as theirs. Not surprising these arseholes grew up to be bigger arseholes, but more on them later. This kind ignorance and wilful disregard for peoples past makes me angry. Though probably not as angry as my real teacher was when he returned to find drawings of Hitler and spitfires on his chalkboard and a stack of untouched maths work.

This stern, cold man let his guard down and allowed us to become part of his past. He didn't have to do this. He simply could have taught the lesson that was left for him but he didn't and I learnt more in those 2 days than all the other classes put together that year. I like to think that he got as much out of those two days as most of us did and I hope that someday people will afford me the time to share my stories with them.

Getting old is no joke, the people you know and love start to fade away and die, the world moves faster and you feel isolated and trapped. You become useless and forgotten, a relic of a time that is no longer relevant and a burden on the young and able. The young could learn a thing or two by taking the time to listen to the voices of experience before they fade away. All too soon the young will become old and they too will pass away taking their memories with them. So no matter how grumpy you are always make time for the incoherent ramblings of your geriatric elders. You might just learn something.

Arseholes

Sorry if you were expecting a clever title or play on words there isn't one for this chapter because this chapter needs to be plain and to the point.

You may recall that somewhere in the introduction to this book I lamented that few people can achieve being an arsehole on a daily basis and that it takes work, dedication and effort. This is true. What I want to discuss now is the fact that there are several different types of arseholes. There's the grumpy arsehole who you should strive to be. They seek out their targets with pin point precision and then unleash a full force of irritating behaviour that will leave their victim a quivering mess in the corner. Then there is the natural arsehole. These are the people who do it in a passive unknowing manner. Without even trying they can become king of the arseholes, but this is not good because it can't be turned off or controlled.

Let me give you a few examples: (beware, broad stereotypes lie ahead)

There are the loud mouthed rich snobs who look down on everyone like they are something nasty they have trodden in. These people are easily spotted. Invariably they have incredibly bad dress sense, awful breath and teeth that could eat an apple through a chain link fence. They burst into a room and immediately demand the full attention and servitude from all those around. They have an air of the upper class twit about them but are so vastly out of touch with the rest of the world that a dose of reality could in fact shock them into an unexpected poverty. They are often born with a silver spoon in their mouths and talk like it's still stuck in there. They are invariably different from the self made rich person who remembers where they have come from and appreciates their own accomplishments. If you remember the old Monty Python sketch called The Upper Class Twit of the Year it encapsulates the character perfectly.

Strangely, you can find a similarly annoying character to this at the lower end of the class scale. They too are loud, obnoxious and ignorant and they generally have a keen interest in football hooliganism. They are often found wearing beer stained vests, jewellery from a high street catalog store and have strong ill-informed views on immigration, the economy and religion.

Many of them display a great enthusiasm for tattoos, usually on the knuckles or neck. They usually holiday in Benidorm and have a wife called Tracey or Bianca. The only silver spoons they have are the ones they have pilfered during their weekly Sunday lunch at Witherspoons.

In between these two extremes you will find the average arsehole. This one is made up of a strange combination of both of the above examples. He often shows no outward signs that he is an arsehole. He blends into society seamlessly, but when you have a conversation with him you will realise very quickly that you are in fact talking directly to an arsehole. They know everything about everything, they have done everything, eaten everything, been everywhere and will correct you on every single thing you say. Their only function in life is to appear better than everyone else. If you buy a nice car, they will come round and tell you it's nice but the colour is wrong, the price was wrong, the model is wrong and really you should have consulted them before you bought. You know full well they know nothing about cars as the roof rack on their grey, nondescript and soulless euro box demonstrates. They will argue the most basic and well established facts until everyone gets fed up and just agrees with them. They feel superior while everyone just mutters to themselves "arsehole."

The type of arsehole you should be aiming for is the quiet, normal, polite and happy go lucky kind. Well-informed, articulate and capable of acknowledging that sometimes you might in fact be wrong but you are always willing to learn. You go through life with your eyes open, observing everything, deciding things for yourself and not falling into the trap of blindly following the herd or doing whats expected. Then when the moment is right and armed with the facts, knowledge and skills built and honed over time, you can execute the most brutal of assaults on your unsuspecting victim. The posh toff will choke on his silver spoon, the loudmouthed hooligan will be beaten into submission and the know it all with the roof rack will be left bereft. You are the wolf in sheep's clothing.

I'm not sure how it is decided which group you fall into, it may be genetic, it may be your upbringing or environment or a combination of the three. One thing is for sure, you will now have an image in your mind of someone you know that fits perfectly into one of these categories. My minds eye is looking at one right now. He was the class bully at school. The loud popular kid. The arrogant one who always knew better. They are often still the same when they are older but life has a great way of levelling the playing field.

Believe it or not growing up I was in the half of the class that made the other half popular. I was quiet and insignificant. Often ignored and overlooked, I contently went about my business in blissful invisibility. I was happy to wait for my turn. It came 3 years after leaving school. It was Christmas and in a small bar a crowd of people had gathered in the warm glow of golden beer while it snowed outside. The mood was happy. The crowd was made up of the normal regulars, a few strangers and lots of former school mates who had returned home for the holidays. During the course of the evening I was approached by a familiar face. I shall simply call him Tarquin. This is not his real name, his real name is Dave but Tarquin encapsulates his personality perfectly. He fitted into toff class of arsehole. This was a cretin of the highest order, a gut wrenching excuse for a human. He used to walk with his head in the air, oblivious to the fact that any of us lower mortals existed. He would have stood on his grandmothers head if he thought it would raise his social standing. The best way to describe him is like a very posh and morally bankrupt yuppie who hadn't quite made it to Wall Street and instead sold cars to those that did.

"Oh wow hey hi ya" he exclaimed with a smile and a wet floppy handshake, "my god how long has it been? What are you up to these days?" he enquired in a bold and loud way that only people like him do. This was my queue. I replied "sorry, do I know you?" "It's me, Taaarrrrquuuinnn" he replied with a look of disbelief on his face. I let the silence carry on just long enough to be awkward. You could see the group of friends he was with starting to look bemused. I began to ask several people who happened to be walking by at the time if they knew who this weirdo was. They looked confused and Tarquin began to look increasingly uncomfortable. Once the awkwardness had played out for a second or two and just as he was about to give up and turn away I shouted "Oh, Tarquin, of course, I remember you". His face regained the smug smile I remembered from all those years ago. After all how could anyone forget him. "I'm great" I said and then he continued to regale me about how much he had achieved since we last met and how he was now gainfully employed as a Personal Executive Transport Procurement Specialist. I think what he actually meant to say was that he sold crappy used cars. At this point he was expecting the social norm to proceed, we would continue to exchange niceties for a moment or two, say it was great to see each other and then move on having confirmed that Tarquin was still at the top of the tree. I had a different plan.

During what appeared to be a hearty parting handshake, I loudly exclaimed "Tarquin, you haven't changed a bit, you're still every bit the arsehole I remember" The conversation in the room died away. Dear Tarquin was going slightly red. I followed this by explaining to his friends who were now listening intently, that our Tarquin had never actually spoken to me before and was in fact a horrible little cretin who made many of my school friends lives utterly miserable. I then informed them that he had the social appeal of a leper colony and they should consider exiling him from their company before he soured the beer.

Tarquin was speechless and now radiating a red glow of embarrassment similar to that of the open fire smouldering in the corner. My similarly ignored school friends cheered which only added to his discomfort. Unable to stomach this rejection and public criticism he briskly left with his silver spoon between his legs. I returned to my corner of the bar and blended back into the sea of faces waiting to be served. Mission accomplished.

A lower standard of arsehole may have just punched the smug faced Tarquin. As satisfying as that would have been, it would have lacked any form of social finesse or acceptability and may have invited undue pity or revenge from the crowd and possibly a spot of tedious litigation from the injured party.

You don't have to be a constant arsehole but when the opportunity presents itself you have to seize it with both hands. Being patient is the key here, you may have to wait years but it's worth it, then you can sink back into obscurity and await the next opportunity to present itself. I could have tackled this cretin years ago, god knows I wanted to but this would have been stupid. Back then he was the king of the jungle surrounded by loyal yes men. I would have been eaten alive. Instead I waited until the jungle was gone. Outside the safe confines of the school he was no longer a somebody but a nobody trying to make his way through life like the rest of us. Life can be unfair and unjust but sometimes it gives you a sweet opportunity to dish out some sour grapes.

Hands Off My Crisps

Have you ever had an urge, an uncontrollable craving, a taste for something that simply must be satisfied. I have. Occasionally I am struck down with an irrepressible need for chocolate. When I am grabbed by this need I cannot focus on anything else, it's like a junkie hunting down his next fix. I would be utterly useless as a spy because if captured I would give up all the state secrets for a bar of Dairy Milk chocolate or a packet of peanut M&Ms.

I've always been a chocolate addict. Even as a young boy I found I could eat vast quantities of the stuff without ever feeling sick or tired of it. When I was younger a bar of chocolate seemed like a meal in itself. Maybe it was just because I was smaller then, but it is difficult to argue with the fact that when I buy a bar of chocolate today I am left with a feeling of profound disappointment. The once huge and satisfying slab of brown goodness now sits in the palm of my hand while I sorrowfully exclaim "Please sir can I have some more?"

You must have noticed this yourself. Almost everything you buy now is about half the size it used to be and costs at least twice as much as it did when I was a lad.

You're probably thinking, "Here we go again. Another old codger ranting on about how you used to be able to go out to the magic moving picture show, buy some popcorn and a drink, get a bag of chips afterwards, pay for a bus fare home and still have change from a fiver." You're wrong, You see prices have to rise with time, it is all part of an expanding and developing economy. Yes, prices are higher but so too are your wages and so too is your standard of living. We all have washing machines, dishwashers and tumble dryers now, and no longer do we have to walk down to the bottom of the garden to have a crap. Unless you are particularly weird and want to or if you are French. As long as I can still earn money I hope prices continue to rise at a steady, reasonable rate and I will budget accordingly. This means living standards will improve.

What I cannot forgive is the practice of shrinking down our products while still putting the prices up. I'm happy to pay 90 of your new pence for my bag of cheese and onion crisps. What angers me beyond belief is when I open the packet to find 6 crisps rattling about in the bottom of the bag and the rest made up of onion flavoured air. If I was suffering from oxygen deprivation at the time I might well be very glad of this waft of onion air but last time I checked the earth was bursting with air. I simply want crisps. An empty wallet I can deal with but an empty belly I simply cannot stomach.

It's not just crisps and the aforementioned chocolate bars that have succumbed to this treachery. Everything from bog roll to biscuits and noodles to napkins are affected. Either the amount in the packet is smaller or the item itself has shrunk to the size that a microscope is needed to unwrap it.

This trend has been noticed by many mainstream media outlets over the years and like everything these days it has to be given a catchy cool moniker. After almost no effort at all they came up with the irritating term Shrinkflation. Truly inspired I think you'll agree, but who is responsible for this modern marvel? We know the Bank of England tries to control inflation by tinkering with interest rates and such things, but I don't believe they are responsible for my shrunken biscuits. Nor do I blame the government for the fact that my bog roll, while still soft and strong, is not quite as long as it used to be. I fear this is the work of the corporate executive.

In a spot of boardroom brainstorming a bright young spark must have floated the idea that they could actually increase profit margins by gradually shrinking their product while charging the same or even more for it. The public would never know. Even if we did catch on what could we do about it. It's like the plot line to some sort of industrial espionage con story or perhaps the precursor to a punchline of a joke between two high powered business people that the average Joe simply isn't privy to. Perhaps they too had been read The Twits by Roald Dahl in school and thought they would copy Mr Twits efforts to make Mrs Twit think she was shrinking. By adding bits of wood to her walking stick and chair she became convinced that she was afflicted by some sort of debilitating disease called the Shrinks. I now feel the inverse of this when eating a Mars bar.

I wonder could I get away with a similar shrinking tactic on my next tax return? Probably not, though i'm pretty confident jail terms have fallen foul to shrinkflation over the years too. See you in 3 to 5 with time off for good behaviour.

Driving Woes and Growing Old

Nothing compares to the unbridled excitement experienced by the teenager in the year or two before they can learn to drive. If you were like me the time between 15 and 17 was excruciating long and painful. All you wanted was the freedom to escape onto the open road. Like me you probably didn't set off in a fire red muscle car across the American route 66 on some sort of voyage of self discovery. A drive along the B316 in a 1989 Peugeot 205 to Tesco for a bottle of coke and a sandwich was about as close as I came to finding myself, but that was enough. Being in control of where you went and when was like opening the flood gates to a brave new world of excitement and discovery. For a brief moment in your short life you were Christopher Columbus sailing off to find land as yet unchartered. Then reality set in and you just drove to work instead. The novelty wore off as quickly as your first set of brake pads.

I look around today and see young people wizzing about in cars, music blaring and exhaust roaring. They drive too aggressively and with the same blatant disregard for other road users as a suicide bomber has for his life insurance payments.

These young whippersnappers think they own the road. They roar around in cars that are modified to the point of stupidity. They skid about reclined in a seating position that's more akin to sunbathing than driving. They spend more time fiddling with their modified knobs than actually concentrating on the task in hand, namely staying between the hedges and not killing anyone.

I know all this is a sweeping generalisation and there are some very responsible young drivers out there but like everything else, it only takes a few to ruin it.

I know that as time moves on these young race drivers will give up their drag racing and doughnutting and take part in less risky car based activities. I read recently that something called dogging was popular amongst older car enthusiasts.

The problem is that these young drivers eventually turn into something much worse... an old driver.

These people are far more of a menace than any young person is behind the wheel. The science backs this up too. As you get older your eyesight and hearing start to fail and as a consequence you drive at a speed slower than stalactite formation. The white lines become irrelevant, especially when in a car park. Old people seem to think it's a competition to park across as many spaces as possible, they abandon their cars rather than park them.

I recently witnessed someone trying to park in my local garden centre car park. There was plenty of room, a row of at least 10 empty spaces lay in front of them just waiting to be filled. They slowed to a speed that allowed slugs to overtake and began to manoeuvre their Nissan Micra directly over the white line of the space. Thankfully they stopped halfway through the manoeuvre to put on their indicators and then continued to a resting position that more resembled an unexpected breakdown than a deliberate attempt at parking. At first I thought this old codger was maybe a former bomber pilot and due to unfortunate senile delusions had become confused and thought he was trying to park his Lancaster after a successful midnight raid on Stuttgart. Without the aid of the guy with the table tennis bats. I expected him to emerge from the cockpit sporting the standard comedy flying goggles and aviators scarf.

The door of the Micra creaked open and a foot fell out. A beige foot, followed by beige trousers and a beige jacket. He pulled a flat cap over his grey head and shuffled off in the direction of the store quite oblivious to the low standard of parking he had achieved or the waiting queues that had amassed behind him.

You see these people quite often on the roads, tootling along like Miss Daisy without a care in the world. They are jittery at junctions, they will wait for ages even when the coast is clear and then pull out exactly when it isn't. They drive at 20mph under the speed limit because they think it's safer and then will swerve across the road or make an unexpected U-turn without so much as a by your leave.

Invariably they believe that they are excellent drivers, why wouldn't they be? They have been driving since 1923 just like the young whippersnapper thinks he's the best driver because he's been driving since 1923 yesterday evening.

I have been the young person behind the wheel and now I'm in that brief moment of life when I can safely and confidently manoeuvre a car without incident. I hope to christ someone has the good sense to remove my wheels before I turn into one of those geriatric flying menaces.

Dinner Is Served

I consider myself to be a fairly modern gentleman. This means I can put a load of soiled pants in the washing machine, run the iron over the carpets and hoover the clothes when they are dry. Easy, I don't know why the other half makes such a fuss about it. I'll even tackle the cooking.

I enjoy cooking and I'm not too bad at it, even if I do say so myself. Granted I'm no Heston Ramsey or Gordon Blumenthal but I can negotiate my way around the kitchen on what could be described as a purely amateur level. Her in doors realised this early on in our relationship and so the cooker became my constant companion.

When I am at home it is taken for granted that I will cook for the family. I don't mind this but as I am a man I like to plan and organise things in advance. Early in the day I will ask the seemingly innocuous question "What does anyone fancy for dinner?" To me this makes sense, but invariably I am greeted with the standard and completely unhelpful response of "whatever".

Great that means it will be my choice. I will plunder through the cupboards and cobble together the ingredients for a delicious meal. I might even make a trip to the shops if I am in a particularly adventurous frame of mind.

Skip forward to about 4pm, I head to the kitchen and start to prepare the dinner. This action must stir some sort of primordial instinct within the teenagers brain. They start to roam into the kitchen and aimlessly poke through the cupboards and fridge. They even look through the cupboards that have no food in them and never had. I presume this is just incase the food mixer that has lay in there, neglected since 1983 has suddenly morphed into a roast chicken or something.

After a few minutes I will enquire as to what they are doing. Apparently they are hungry. I explain that as they can surely see I am making dinner and it will be ready in about half an hour. This is met with cries of bewilderment and despair. "Half an hour, but I'm hungry now". I explain that the chances of them dropping dead from starvation in the next 30 minutes are in fact minuscule and that their chances of death are virtually guaranteed if they do not leave the kitchen immediately. I find that holding a 12 inch kitchen knife in my hand as I explain this usually aids in their rapid departure. They strop off to some unexplored end of the house to nibble on a handful of biscuits that they swiped when my back was turned and I continue to cook.

Glass of wine in hand and an old episode Top Gear usually playing in the background for company, I stir, turn and flip the food until I am satisfied that all traces of salmonella have been abolished. I set the table and adorn it with all the condiments one could desire. I pour the drinks and carefully position the food on the plates. I put the utmost care into ensuring that dinner will be a dignified and pleasurable experience and then I yell "DINNERS ON THE TABLE!!!"

Without fail those who had been at deaths door with starvation not half an hour ago seem to be in no rush whatsoever to eat, instead the dog usually arrives first, keen to get first dibs on whatever she can.

Eventually people start to filter to the table in dribs and drabs. I watch as different items of food then get shoved to one side of the plate.

Then comes the barrage of inevitable questions. "Why are there vegetables on my plate? You know I hate vegetables." "Why can't we have proper food in this house?" "This is too spicy, and I wanted chips". Nothing and I mean nothing can ever be right. If I make fish they want steak, if I make steak they want fish. It's a battle that can never be won. You hope that perhaps the evening can be saved with some polite dinner conversation but that too is just a pipe dream. The bickering and quarrelling usually ends in some form of grievous bodily harm with intent, but then thats probably my fault. After all I was the one that armed them with the knife and fork in the first place.

I sit there in a puddle of sweat, blood boiling and head pounding while the condensation of the last half hours work is dripping from the ceiling. By this stage the notion of eating has completely left me and I vow never again to enter the kitchen.

After 10 minutes all the food has been shovelled away, plates are scraped and the people filter off to the various rooms of the house from which they came. I sit there wondering what's just happened. Surrounded by dirty dishes and with pots and pans piled high in the sink, the clean up begins. After an hour or so the kitchen is as good as new and there are no signs of the slaughter that took place earlier. Dinner in my house is to be endured rather than enjoyed.

I grab the remainder of the bottle of wine or pour a small whisky and return to my chair in the sitting room.   I sink down deep into its comfortable cushions and recline back, a moment or two passes then like a brick to the face I get hit with it...

"What's for dinner tomorrow?"

I inwardly clutch my chest as the pain starts to take hold, my insides are screaming but calmly and with no outward sign of distress I turn and ask "What would you like?"

Who The Hell Is Jim?

To me there is nothing more disgusting than spending time in a room surrounded by other peoples sweaty arse cracks while they grunt and groan pulling muscles and stupid faces, but it seems to have become a national pastime.

Gyms are everywhere you look now. People go there before work, at lunchtime and again after work. They even make time on their day off work to go back again. There are even apps to tell you where your closest gym is incase you are suddenly struck down with a debilitating urge to lift something heavy. It is big business, billions are spent on gym memberships, equipment, clothing, protein drinks and healthy living snacks every year. For the life of me I just can't fathom what the appeal is.

I remember when gyms were the preserve of the rich, the yuppie squash player and Arnold Schwarzenegger. No one else was welcome and no one else cared.

I'm not, as you may have guessed a big fan of the gym. Curiosity did once get the better of me and I went to see what all the fuss was about.

I drove down to my local leisure centre and confidently stated to the girl behind the desk that I was here to see gym and could she point me in his direction. Having put on my newly acquired gym gear there could be no doubt that I certainly looked the part. I instantly blended in with 70% of the people there, lost, bewildered and slightly fatter than is deemed healthy for your age. I will discuss the other 30% in more detail later.

I was introduced to a young man called Jason. He stood there like some sort of chiseled adonis, immaculately groomed and looking cool. He was enthusiastic and eagerly started asking all sorts of intrusive questions about my diet and long term fitness goals. He wanted to draw up some sort of meal plan and sign me up to a years subscription of cardio and core strength development. I politely said no but I would appreciate if he could show me how to use some of the quite frankly torturous looking equipment. Jason's spark had left him. He realised I wasn't a true gymanite and wasn't going to be funding his avocado lifestyle through a monthly subscription to his motivational madness. He reluctantly pointed and said, "There's the treadmill, thats the weights area, here are the rowing machines and thats the cross trainer." I was inches away from making a quip about him being the only cross trainer I could see but I thought it best not to. He had developed a somewhat displeased and disappointed look about him and a bulging vein was twitching dangerously on his left temple. It was obvious I was not welcome here. I decided it was best to let him return to his corner and continue checking his hairstyle in the mirror.

I sat myself down on a somewhat disturbingly damp and slippery contraption and aimlessly began to row. As I wasn't actually going anywhere and was getting a little bored, I decided to have a look around at the other people puffing and panting on the various torture machines this place had on offer.

As I mentioned before a lot of them looked like me, they were here for some reason but they were not really 100% sure what that reason was. Then there was the other 30%. These are the people that put people like me off going to these places. There were angry, serious people who looked like they would kill you if you even thought about disturbing their intense workout. It was almost as if their life depended on it or something. Then there were the posers, these people looked good. They had all the gear and trendy water bottles to match but not one of them had a bead of sweat on them. Wireless earphones in, they wandered from machine to machine casually looking at themselves from all angles in the big mirrors that made up most of the walls in the place. These people seemed to be here to either show off, socialise or attract a mate. Some seemed to spend more time engaged in a one person photoshoot with their phone than actually doing any form of exercise.

A series of loud animal like noises drew my attention away from the beautiful people and onto a very strange group of animals in the far corner of the room. These people I can only describe as muscle bound freaks with square shoulders and heads to match. They seemed to hang out exclusively in the weights area. These knuckle draggers were to be avoided at all costs. They grunted and groaned like apes as they lifted the heaviest weight they could find, once, and then dropped it to the ground and walked away staring into the distance. I thought there maybe was a TV or something very interesting on a distant wall, but I checked and as far as I could see there was nothing. This hundred yard stare seemed to be part of their workout routine. It was during one of these walking stares that I observed a strange trait that all of these apes possessed. They all walked like they had suffered some form of embarrassing trouser accident. They took tiny shuffling steps while keeping their entire upper body as solid and straight as possible. It looked terribly uncomfortable, painful even.

After half an hour or so I had tried most of the activities the room had to offer and I was utterly bored. Bored of the continuous and monotonous movements and matching music. Bored of the chilled air conditioning blasting all around me like a breath from Jack Frost himself. I was bored of the apes and their grunts, bored of the posers and their Instagram photos, bored of the rejection and condescending looks of disapproval from the serious gym enthusiasts but most of all, I was bored with all the sweating and chaffing. So I left.

As I left the windowless air conditioned torture emporium behind I was greeted by something strange. A big bright world full of space and fresh air. People were out walking, kids were playing football and apart from a few militant cyclists in lycra, all these people were getting exercise in a very enjoyable and leisurely manner.

This was my moment of clarity but I had to venture into the depths of hell and suffer all its demons to realise the wonders of heaven.

I still visit the gym but when I get there I turn around and walk home again. No grunting apes, no pressure to look good and no sweaty arse crack to deal with. Jim can sod off.

Old Bones, Creaks and Groans

Last Friday I went out for a drink. Not much unusual about that you might say and you would be right. It was a very tame and grown up sort of an evening. Polite conversation flowed over a few beers until a couple of civilised whiskeys finished off the night around midnight. Then home and into bed. There was no slurred speech, no one fell over, no arguments or fights and not even one drink was spilt. So whats the big deal? The fact of the matter is that 3 days later I am still recovering. The pneumatic drill that I woke up with bouncing uncontrollably around my head the next day has now settled to a dull ache that has taken up residence just behind my eyeballs. My stomach is still reluctant to accept food of any kind and I am haunted by a nauseous spirit that drapes a feeling of dread and fear over me like some sort of debilitatingly heavy cloak of sweat. My tongue feels like the rough end of a badger and there simply isn't enough water in the country to quench my thirst.

A few years ago I could have knocked back 10 times this and been bright as a button by lunchtime the next day, eaten a small horse for dinner and then headed out to do the same thing all over again. This was normal and was in fact my daily routine during the student years. Those days I fear are long gone. If I was to attempt a night out of those proportions now I would undoubtably end up in a morgue before 10pm.

It isn't just my ability to cope with the horrors of drink that have taken a downward turn over the last few years. I have noticed other things too. My movements and reactions have slowed to that of a sloth. I used to be able to get up, get ready for work and be in the car within 10 minutes of my alarm going off, now it takes me 10 minutes just to muster enough energy to get both feet out of the bed. I used to eat whatever I wanted whenever I wanted. Now even the smell of food after 8pm will leave me bloated and incapable of getting a solid nights sleep, not to mention the fire that rages in my stomach if I actually do eat something before bed. I now have to take a tablet to control my wayward digestive juices as well as a multi-vitamin to help my joints move me throughout the day. The kids are out popping pills for a good time while I'm at home popping pills to survive.

I used to have a TV in my living room. It has now been replaced by some sort of magic sleep machine. I have my dinner in the evening then sit myself down in front of this little box and within minutes I am out like a light, dead to the world, snoring and with a slight dribble running down my chin. At one stage I suspected that the wife was trying to bump me off by dumping sleeping pills in my food but she insists that I'm just old and done.

Life really has taken a turn for the worse.

You may have noticed that some of these things are happening to you. You may have discussed it with friends or maybe even your doctor. They likely advised something radical like taking in some more exercise or improving your diet. This is fine if that is what you want to do but I have given it some thought and this is my solution to the problem. DO NOTHING.

Let me tell you why. I have spent my entire life to this point working and toiling away just to live a reasonable life. I have been through the drinking and partying stage and I am now content to leave that in the past.

Spending the evening standing in a loud and noisy pub straining to hear what someone two feet away from you is saying, fighting to get a drink at the bar and then assaulting my digestive system with some meat of questionable origin before trying to make my way home surrounded by drunken arseholes no longer appeals to me. I am quite content to sit quietly in my chair at home, warm and relaxed sipping on a drink that no one is going to knock out of my hand or spike. Then I can go to bed at a reasonable time and wake up in the morning a fully functioning human ready to cope with whatever the day wishes to throw at me.

My creaky bones and three day hangovers serve as a great reminder that my body has moved out of its guarantee period and that I should be content to take things a little easier. Leave the young ones to party and rush about and pretty soon they too will find that life will inevitably catch up with them.

Accept this knowledge and be content with your ageing body. All the creeks and groans that come from it are merely a sign that a life has been lived but there is still some life in the old dog yet. Eating vegetables and doing sit ups will only irritate your already worn body. Sit down, relax and enjoy a well deserved break.

You Do What For A Living?

Unless you have been living under a rock you have probably noticed a trend that has developed over the past few years of renaming old jobs with exciting new dynamic titles. For example we used to have bin men, they emptied the bins. It was a much needed and under appreciated job and I gather it was quite well paid too. It was all quite simple and straight forward, now we have Household Waste Management and Disposal Technicians. It sounds very grand and fluffy and apparently politically correct but I think their main duties still involves emptying the bins. We used to have the much maligned Traffic Warden who gave out tickets to people who couldn't park correctly. Now we have what is called a Parking Enforcement Officer. They sound like they will club you over the head, drag you into the back of a waiting van and promptly throw you in some far of gulag never to be seen again.

Librarians are Literature Information Assistants. Communication Executives are those annoying people in call centres that call you up at inappropriate times to be helpful but are usually very unhelpful when you return the favour and call them with a question. Accountants have become Financial Asset Analysts, the tax man is a Debt Management Officer and an insurance sales man is a Family and Property Protection Specialist. Even the guy that works on the line at a chicken factory is called a Critical Process Operative. It's all bollocks.

In a world full of Forward Data Liaison Officers, Principal Marketing Assistants and Dynamic Configuration Facilitators it can be difficult to know what anyone actually does for a living. Most of them probably don't know themselves but it sounds impressive and important when they're talking to people in the pub.

Most of these things don't really bother me that much. You can call yourself whatever you want for all I care, but one job on this earth that really bothers me is the Customer Recruitment and Procurement Specialist. Or CRAPS for short. Have you ever heard of them? I bet you will have come across them plenty of times. Their normal stomping ground is outside the bars, restaurants and nightclubs of popular foreign holiday towns. These are the people who are employed by an establishment to stand on the street outside and annoy, badger and harass those passing by.

My first experience of these people occurred on the island of Tenerife. A bunch of us went there for a lads holiday not long after we had been released from compulsory education. At first it was quirky and somewhat of a novelty. All these people offering exclusive discounts into their bar, free drinks all round and promises of exclusive VIP treatment. This became tedious very quickly, so much so that by day three of the holiday one of our party had cracked. Towards the end of the night this normally upstanding and somewhat decent member of the community began launching beer bottles at an unfortunate and rather unsuspecting procurement specialist. Forcing a few surprised holidaymakers who unwittingly found themselves caught in the crossfire to take cover behind some nearby palm trees. Luckily his aim was somewhat off as he had already drank the contents of the bottles before throwing them. Unfortunately for us this was the time before camera phones and so this escapade was never caught on tape. He could have been the next big viral internet sensation or at the very least we could have tortured him with the footage for years to come.

Today when I go on holiday and get harassed every 10 paces by one of these happy, joyful irritating individuals, I can feel reality drift away for a second. I contemplate the beer bottle in my hand and think what it would look like flying through the air, but thats not the behaviour one would expect from a Creative Syntactical Engineer or an Executive Linguistic Choreographer.

The Mediterranean Oil Slick

We all know the typical salesman persona. Slick, greasy, full of charm, conversational wit and something else that rhymes with wit. Typically they can be found selling used cars or double glazing but they can also be found peddling all manner of commodities like insurance, speciality mops and indeed the smart wifi kettle mentioned in a previous chapter.

I've had the misfortune to deal with most of these types of people in my life as I'm sure you have too, but today I witnessed greasy salesmanship on an unprecedented level. Let me set the scene for you. It is currently 18 degrees, the sun is shinning and the temperature is climbing towards the mid twenties.

The small English owned cafe on the Costa del Sol in which I am currently sitting, is a pleasant place to be. Here I can enjoy a traditionally cooked Full English breakfast and a cup of tea. Both of which have a strong film of grease on top. Today though the grease is not confined to the plate of fried eggs and sausage that sits in front of me. At the table across from me sits a man wearing ill-fitting black trousers and a casual shirt with one too many buttons open. His hair is slicked back with enough oil to lubricate the engine on the Titanic and his mobile phone is clipped to his belt. His bluetooth ear piece sits in his ear like he is receiving constant communications directly from corporate HQ. Across the table from him an elderly couple sit. After a short while I begin to realise what I am actually witnessing is in fact some kind of holiday hostage situation. Hemmed in against the wall by the breakfast table and the unbearable manner of this human oil slick, the elderly couple gingerly nibble on the fried rations provided by their captor.

My attention was drawn to the seemingly constant onslaught of sales speak and corporate bullshit this guy was bamboozling the elderly couple with. He was certainly at the top of his game. He was in fact a timeshare salesman. The worst of all the sales people. Like most people who are involved in sales or marketing, he too seemed incapable of holding a conversation at any sort of normal volume. He was just the sort of person I would usually have the misfortune of being stuck beside on a train or long haul flight.

He sat there conning these poor people out of their life savings. They sat there agreeing with everything this man said. He rhymed off the benefits of the Platinum Membership Package and the need for their special Essential Corporate Insurance cover should one of them die. Incidentally he was uniquely placed to offer them a one time discount should they wish to sign on the dotted line today. They nodded in agreement as he spewed out how his company was simply better than anyone else in the business. They had invested millions into their products and services over the past number of years and now they could provide simply the best personally tailored holiday solution anyone could want. Call me a cynic but I was skeptical.

The real cherry on the cake came when he regaled them with the story of a nice couple he knew, strangely, quite similar to themselves he claimed. The husband, Colin, had spent years diligently putting money away for a rainy day, they lived a modest life and went on modest holidays. Now retired they wanted to enjoy life. Stupidly they thought they could save a few quid and purchased one of the lower cost schemes that an inferior competitor had been flogging.

Then bang the husband died while staying at some godforsaken rat infested bedsit in Tenerife.

The poor wife, Sheila, didn't know what to do. She ran up and down the hallway banging on doors and begging for help as her husband lay on the floor clutching his chest. She didn't speak Spanish and there was no concierge available because of the cheap inferior product they had unwittingly purchased. He actually suggested that had they bought his product her husband may well still have been alive. At this point I nearly threw my bacon at him. He was actually suggesting that he was the saviour of all men, and while having some money in the bank was ok, it would be much better not to leave anything for surviving relatives or grieving widows. Much better to give it all to him today and enjoy superior holidays because after all you cant take it with you. He was using fear to browbeat these poor pensioners into parting with their life savings, after all they didn't want to end up like the foolish Colin and Shiela in his Tenerife tale.

As my blood boiled at the ferocity of his unscrupulous sales tactics, I became distracted by another loud speaking english man by the door of the cafe. Another oil slick had slid in and was about to put another unsuspecting couple through the wringer. He reamed off much the same story and used the same tactics as the first guy. Half an hour later a third bastard had shuffled in yet another unsuspecting couple. The small terrace was now covered on three sides by these corporate bullshit merchants. It was enough to put me right off my breakfast.

There was no option but to make a break for it before they broke off into some sort of pincer movement and nabbed my life savings too. Now, three hours later I'm lying on a sun lounger with the waves lapping gently at my feet. However my mind cannot get away from the poor souls in the cafe being filled with bacon and eggs while their pockets were being emptied of all they had worked for in life. This was just one cafe in one small corner of the world for one hour on a random Tuesday morning in late May. The sums of cash being discussed were by no means insignificant. These vultures must be fleecing hundreds of thousands of pounds a month from people in cafes up and down the coast. You may think there is nothing wrong with this, that it is simply the cut and thrust of the business world and the application of free market economics. Anyway, the customers were fully functioning adults and quite capable of making their own decisions. This may well all be true, but imagine if it was your parents sitting across from one of these vipers, being subjected to high pressure sales techniques and tales of death and despair. You would happily drown the cretinous little snake in his greasy cup of tea.

I'm sure there are some very honest and conscientious sales people out there who do generally want what is best for their customers. However I have yet to met one such person. My opinion is that most people in the sales business have no scruples at all and will happily take you for every penny you own if you let them. I only hope that when I am older and probably more senile than I am now, I will still have the clarity of mind to tell these greased vipers to eff off, but only after they've filled me with bacon and eggs first.

The Final Cut

If you are like me you will enjoy and appreciate a good sensible hair cut. There is nothing better than getting a good neat tidy up in the follicle department.

As a man I do not need an accomplished award winning stylist, nor do I require a 3 hour long appointment to take care of the task in hand or to pay £100 for the privilege of having someone else wash and dry my hair. A simple short back and sides is all that is required.

Having tried numerous barbers over the years I have experienced all manner of irritating disappointments and unpleasantness. A few years back I was next in line for my usual trim when the guy in the chair got up and angrily stormed over to the door and locked it. Trapping everyone inside while he began ranting and raving at the barber. At first I thought I had become involved in some sort of hairdresser hijacking debacle but after a lot of arm waving and pointing it became clear that the customer believed the barber was on some form of psychedelic drug. You would have thought the same if you had seen what he had done to the poor mans hair.   Anyway the manager was summoned and it was explained that the young barber was not high on an exotic tobacco but was in fact a diabetic and was low blood sugar. This was causing him to shake in a manner not conducive to holding a set of sharpened steel blades millimetres from a human head. I may be wrong but I suspect the strong smell of alcohol seeping from his pores may have had something to do with his condition. The young barber was dispatched to get some fresh air and Lucozade while the manager set about trying to fix the unhappy customers barnet. In any case it was a close shave for me. It was time to search for a new barber.

With the proliferation of mens hair boutiques these days you would think this would be an easy task, but you would be wrong. The first one I tried always had a queue of at least 5 or 6 people in front of you. Worse still they catered for children. Colourful car shaped chairs were employed to distract the screaming brats from the razor sharp pieces of metal being waved frantically around their struggling and reluctant heads.   It was like combining a third rate amusement arcade with an abattoir. It was a blood bath waiting to happen. The third red flag this place had involved the thumping pop music they insisted on pumping out at what can only be described as nightclub levels. Though this may have just been a vain attempt by the management to mask the screams of the tortured toddlers. Instead of being a relaxing experience, getting a hair cut here was like sticking your head in a cement mixer full of razor blades while a delinquent child kicked you about the back off the knees. Further searching was required.

Onward to the next place. This was a quieter setting, a single TV played in the corner at a reasonable level, the queues always seemed minimal and the hair cuts were quick and neat. However, suitable as this place appeared to be it had one major downfall. They insisted on having the same inane conversation over and over again with you on every visit. It usually started with "so you not working today?" and then progressed through the usual tedious topics of the weather, holidays and my plans for the rest of the day. Instead of being a relaxing experience, getting a hair cut here was like the Spanish inquisition. Even with the comfy chair it simply would not do. The search continued.

I tried numerous barbers, one was even above a butchers shop that made very tasty pies but I always felt a tad uneasy going in there. Flashbacks of Sweeney Todd flooded my mind when the blades came out to do my neck.

Eventually I was running out of places to go and I was in dire need of a trim. As luck would have it I was in town early one morning and happened to park outside a barbers shop I hadn't seen before. The neon sign in the window shimmered like an oasis in the desert. I went in. I was greeted by a row of empty seats and a small jolly man who welcomed me like a long lost friend. He shook my hand, took my coat, hung it up and ushered me into the most comfortable barbers chair I have ever sat in. The Italian leather smelt brand new and the rich marble counter in front of me shone under the soft and carefully placed mood lighting. Mirrors adorned the walls with recessed LED lights providing a rich and relaxing ambience over the spotless sinks that lined the wall like soldiers on parade. The barber, who introduced himself as Denis in a thick Turkish accent, showed the utmost attention to detail, no hair was left uncut, precision was the name of his game. He talked no more than what was relevant to the job in hand and avoided any irritating and unnecessary small talk. After about 20 minutes of fastidious work he announced that he was finished. The cape that was taped around my neck was removed in the same manner an Italian waiter waves a napkin. My coat was retrieved from the peg and held up in a way that allowed my arms to fall into it. I paid my bill which was reasonable, was thanked for choosing his barbers shop and extended an invitation to please call again. I was even presented with a loyalty card. I had found it, a barbering heaven in a sea of hacks and cutthroats. My quest for a suitable haircut was over.

I've been back to this barber every month for the past 6 months and not one bad experience have I had, that is until the Turkish army got involved.

On my last visit young Denis was not his usual focused self. He was distracted by a large brown envelope on the counter. In an unusual move he broke professional standards and engaged in conversation. He said he was in trouble. The army was after him. Needless to say I was intrigued. Was Denis some sort of international spy or double agent? Was he deep undercover and just masquerading as a simple barber? Was

Denis even his real name? Who was this disciplined and efficient man, highly proficient in the handling of sharpened blades?

Turns out Denis was not the Turkish Jason Bourne or even the Turkish Austin Powers. Turns out he had not yet completed his military service and the Turks were not best pleased. Denis was between a rock and a hard place. Did he leave the business and the life he had travelled halfway around the world to build and return to serve in an army he no longer recognised as being his own or should he simply ignore the request? Choosing the latter option meant that he could never return home to visit his family because as soon as he presented himself at the border he would be bundled into a jeep, given a crew cut and taken off to begin his basic training.

Young Denis has a real predicament on his hands but I just hope he takes into consideration the considerable strife I will have to endure if I have to find another new barber. Maybe i'd suit long hair, how long can the army keep you for anyway?

Sour Faced Gits

You have probably guessed that I enjoy a bit of comedy now and again. I don't have much time for people with no sense of humour. We all know someone who is constantly in serious mode, no room for joy or outward displays of happiness. They trudge about with a face that looks like a 10lb bag of fertiliser and have a personality to match.

You will find these people hiding everywhere. With their stern looks of disapproval and eye rolling at the mere hint of jocularity, they can seriously ruin your day.

God help you if you happen to work with one of these people. If just one of them infiltrates your workforce it can make your 30 year career seem like a life sentence with no hope of parole. A great miserableness will infect everyone around, you will age quicker, life will become a chore and the whole workplace will be draped in a heavy blanket of drizzle and despair.

Luckily where I work, we plough on regardless. Practical jokes and pranks are around every corner. It almost makes going to work worthwhile and enjoyable. With persistence you can break down these miserable people and remould them into something that resembles a real human being.

Let me walk you through some of the things my colleagues get up to that make my job tolerable.

Firstly we have the annoying but relatively tame practical jokes. Ink secreted on the handles of doors or desk drawers is a firm favourite, especially when deployed in a persistent and sustained manner. It can go on relentlessly for days and provide hours of giggles. Especially when the boss decides to grace us with one of their impromptu walkabouts, leaving the frustrated victim trying desperately to hide his hands in fear of having to explain why they look as like a Dulux colour chart. It can reduce grown men to a bag of nerves. Swapping out black ink pens in the stationary cupboard with red refills can also provide a delayed and indiscriminate stationery attack.

If your office has a kitchen you are really in luck. A hot chilli pepper cut in half and rubbed around the lip of the bosses coffee mug will lift the mood of the entire office for days not to mention his blood pressure too. We have also developed a game called The Russian Roulette Teabag. If there are any tea drinkers in the office, make a very small incision in one of their tea bags then using an empty pen as a funnel, dump some salt inside the bag and secrete it back in the tea box. Weeks can pass before it gets used but when it does the results are spectacular. For a more immediate and widespread effect just dump a handful straight into the sugar bowl, just remember not to use it yourself unless your are attempting some form of elaborate technique to deflect blame onto someone else.

Remember some efforts will fail but persistence is the key.

One trick that was tried and seemed to fail at first but then worked out better than we ever could have hoped for, involved slicing up some chicken stock cubes into wafer thin pieces and placing them inside the ham sandwiches of an unsuspecting colleague. We eagerly waited as he took his first bite. No response, a second bite was taken but still nothing. The whole sandwich was consumed with no reaction whatsoever. We concluded that years of overindulgent alcohol consumption had killed his taste buds. The prank appeared to have been a failure. However the following day at lunch we found our colleague staring disappointedly at his sandwich. Apparently he had gone home the day before and praised his wife for the tremendous sandwiches she had made for him. He said that in the last 30 years of marriage they had been the best she had ever made, full of flavour and an absolute joy to eat. He requested that she never buy the usual cheap ham again instead she was to buy this new heavenly ham no matter what the cost. He had tasted heaven and there was no way he was going back to the regular stuff the peasants have to eat.

She of course had no idea what he was rabbiting on about and thought he was being facetious. This caused some disgruntlement in his household that night. Now everyday he reminisces over the perfect ham sandwich that his wife simply refuses to make for him again.

If you were starting to feel sorry for this old man, don't, he was one of the biggest clowns and pranksters in the place. One of his trademark moves was to keep a small syringe of warm water in his pocket. He would then lie in wait until you were involved in some deep discussion with a customer. Then he would strike. The tip of syringe would be discreetly placed in the pocket of the unsuspecting employee and the warm liquid would be injected deep into their trousers. At this stage he had 2.5 to 3 seconds to make his retreat and then look on in amusement as the victim began to feel the first dribble of warm water run down their inside leg. Nothing will ever come close to the look of fear on a grown mans face when he believes he has suffered a water based trouser accident in public. He is now left with two options, continue on as best he can until he can excuse himself from the situation and discreetly dash to the toilet to check his trousers, or he can stand proudly and announce to the customer that he may have in fact just pissed himself. Which option would you pick?

Sticking with the watery end of things, polystyrene cups filled with water and attached precariously to the inside of cupboard doors will also attract lots of laughs when they are opened, dousing the unsuspecting victim from head to toe. Just remember to put out the wet floor signs after or health and safety might get involved and they spoil everything. Rotten eggs and rancid tinned fish stashed in drawers or cupboards are also a firm favourite. There is nothing as unpleasant or frustrating as being forced to spend your working day in the presence of a putrid odour, the source of which cannot be found. Long exposure to this means that the smell often sticks in your nose and you find yourself sitting at home later that evening convinced that someone has secreted a kipper under your sofa.

No one is off limits in these escapades. Our boss announced one morning that she would be having lunch with a close personal friend that afternoon and would be late back to the office. Clandestine operations immediately sprang into action and informant shakedowns commenced. Where was she going? Who with and what time the table was booked for? Information is power when orchestrating such devious plans but never gather it directly incase the victim puts 2 and 2 together and comes up with you as the culprit. Anyway, a phone number was sourced for the restaurant and instructions had been left with the staff that an important client was being taken to lunch. A good impression was needed and it was requested that a bottle of their finest champagne was to be opened and waiting for them on arrival. This of course led to all sorts of embarrassment when the bill was to be settled, not least when the company accountant began questioning why he should be paying for champagne lunches.

Pranks inevitably escalate and you have to be ready to always go one step further than the last person. We have had peoples cars advertised for sale, lorry loads of sand dumped on peoples driveways, fertiliser spread on colleagues gardens when they have been on holiday. They just cannot believe how their grass has grown to waist height in 2 weeks. All manner of things have been stuck on, hung from or placed inside each others car. Fresh tuna pushed into the radiator grill works like a charm. The most recent attack saw a pair of men's XXXL white underpants filled with a mixture of brown sauce, wet coffee granules and well placed teabag stains suspended from the back wiper of the bosses car. The addition of appropriately stained bog roll only added into its authenticity. This caused much amusement to the people in the cars behind her and to the few hundred people in the town centre as she drove home with shitty underpants and bog roll flying like a flag from the back of her posh german saloon.

Without doubt the best pranks are the most dangerous ones. The sort that could get you fired on the spot. One of my colleagues who we shall call "Mr B" to protect his identity and preserve any dignity he may have left by the end of this is one man who knows no fear.

Mr B is a larger than life character and a very likeable bloke, he is of an age that you would expect him to behave in a grown up and mature manner, but like the rest of us he is still a big kid. Unfortunately Mr B suffers from extreme bouts of the most horrendous and putrid flatulence. It is truly horrific but he loves nothing more than to inflict his horrible intestinal gas on those around him. On one very boring Tuesday afternoon he had an expulsion of gas that surpassed all previous farts known to man. Let me explain the manner in which he did it. I was at my desk talking quietly with the only client in the office at the time. Mr B was sitting not more than 3 feet way at the desk next to us. I noticed out of the corner of my eye that he was moving his chair closer and closer to my desk. Much to my peril I ignored this move. My client was busy filling out a form on the desk in front of him when Mr B struck. His plan was to kneel backwards on his office chair and then spin himself in my direction. He hoped that his spin would bring his arse to rest inches from the left side of my face but he over cooked it. My client looked up from his paperwork to the sight of Mr B's ample rear end staring him straight in the face. Before the poor man could comprehend what was happening Mr B released an almighty gust of arse wind straight into his face at point blank range. I have never witnessed a man's face express so many emotions at one time. Mr B calmly stood up, adjusted his trousers and walked off without saying a single word or in any way acknowledging what he had just done.

The two of us just sat there completely silent surrounded by a pungent smell that was so thick you could have bitten into it. Neither of us said a word, we sat there looking at each other for what seemed like an eternity, waiting to see who would react first. Now I had a choice to make. I could apologise profusely and hope for the best, or dig deep into my soul and try to muster up the most sincere poker face of my life and continue on as if nothing had happened. There was a chance, small as it was, that my client would have gone along with this approach, if not out of embarrassment then out of sheer disbelief. I was struggling to keep it together and there was no way that I could keep a straight face. My client could see my predicament and threw me a lifeline. He asked in a comedy french accent "did he just fart in my general direction?" This reference to a famous Monty Python sketch and the glimmer in his eyes showed me that he was in fact a man of humour. We both recoiled in gut grabbing laughter and tears streamed down our faces as the pungent odour dissipated throughout the room.

This situation could have been disastrous had the client been one of those joyless serious people I talked about at the start of this chapter. So remember no matter how grumpy you are or how badly the world gets you down always take time to laugh and look for the humour in everything. I have a plaque hanging on my kitchen wall it reads "Don't take life too seriously, no one gets out alive anyway". A flippant comment it may be but soberingly true.

Falling Into The Abyss

Some people believe in heaven and hell, some people believe in reincarnation and some people believe in absolutely nothing. No matter what you believe you are basing it on nothing more than blind faith. For centuries scholars, explorers, professors and theologians have searched religious sites, poured over countless religious texts, peered deep into the earth and the outer reaches of space in search for any hard physical evidence that could either prove or disprove the theories of religion.

After thousands of years of searching and countless religious wars I can confidently announce that I have seen definitive proof that hell actually exists.

It happened on an innocuous Wednesday evening in early March. The sky was clear and crisp and the first signs of spring could be seen on the stark branches in the hedgerows. I was barrelling along nicely making my way to the docks after a training seminar that turned out to be less tedious than expected. The evening sun rested just above the horizon casting a pleasant glow through the window, traffic was light and I was making excellent time for the boat trip home. Billy Joel was playing his piano on my dashboard and all was right with the world.

Then as life would usually have it, fate kicks you up the arse exactly when you least expect it. It came in the form of a loud bang followed by a shuddering jolt. It felt like the entire bowels of the car had fallen out, as did mine. I came to an abrupt halt. I sat for a second contemplating what had just happened. Eventually after my legs had stopped shaking and my white knuckles could be prised off the steering wheel I got out. At first I could see nothing wrong but as I rounded the passenger side of the car I saw it.

I had never seen anything like it, it was awe inspiring. I stood there speechless for a good couple of minutes just staring at it in disbelief. The darkness seemed to stretch on forever, right to the centre of the earth, right into hell itself. I swear I could hear demonic laughter echoing from deep down in this yawning hole in the road.

My wheel had had it, probably the shock absorber too I was lucky the whole car wasn't swallowed up by this huge gap in the earths crust.

I sat on the grass verge contemplating this gateway to hell that I had driven into. As the last of the sunlight faded below the tree line and the yellow glow of the recovery truck appeared in the distance, I asked myself where a hole like this could have come from? It can't have just appeared overnight and I was sure I wasn't its only victim. Other motorists must have made the same journey and nearly fell into Lucifer's living room, but ultimately I asked why me?

The helpful mechanic shook his head and sighed. I was a sight he had seen all too often. As he removed my buckled and distorted wheel he entertained me with numerous comforting facts. Facts like I was two and a half times more likely to suffer a pothole related accident than I was 10 years ago and that on average local government employees repair a pothole every 17 seconds. As you can imagine this warmed the cockles of my heart to the same degree that my supper would be by the time I eventually got home.

Anyway after a while my wheel was replaced but the news wasn't good news for the shock absorber. It was drivable but only just. This meant a trip to the local garage but thats a saga for another time.

As the helpful travelling mechanic trundled off to rescue another broken motorist from their own personal hell hole, I set off home to rescue what remained of my supper. In a darker and hungrier mood my thoughts returned to the hole from which I had just been rescued.

The fact is that there is no money to fix our crumbling roads, the government is all but broke. The purse strings have had to be tightened since a few greedy and irresponsible bankers got trigger happy handing out mortgages to people who had no hope of ever paying them back. This was the credit crisis of 2008. This was why I was sat in a hedge on a Wednesday evening with my car wheel wedged in the devils ass crack like some sort of hellish bike rack. The greed of a Wall Street yuppie over a decade ago set about a devilish chain of events that would culminate in me missing my supper on the 6th March in a 6 inch hole on the A666 just outside Bolton.

Greed certainly is one of the 7 deadly sins but why should I, the humble motorist, be punished for it?

The devil certainly does exist and he doesn't seem to like us putting tarmac all over his roof.

Your Spleen Needs A Service

After the motoring debacle outlined in the previous chapter I was left with the need to visit my mechanic. Truth be told, I would prefer to deep fry my own face than visit my mechanic. I hate going to the garage. It is one of the few places that even the most confident and manly of men are placed entirely at the mercy of the oily spanner clutcher and his diagnosis. He can reduce you to tears by the enormous bill that he knows he can charge you because the only other option you have is to give up the car and walk. No one will do this, ever.

Like most people my mechanical knowledge is somewhat lacking. I know that petrol goes in one end, a series of small explosions happen at the front end, a few pistons move and just like most animals, what's left over comes out the back of it. I can change a bulb and put air in the tyres but ask me to do anything more than that and you might as well be asking me to do quantum physics while wrestling an alligator.

This gap in my knowledge means that should my mechanic be having a slow week he could simply tell me that all manner of things needed to be done to keep my much needed car on the road. Who wants to be the guy that knew better than the expert only to return a week or so later with a broken car and their wheels between their legs.

Thankfully my mechanic seems to be largely trustworthy but on occasion I have had the need to attend other establishments for urgent repairs. About a year ago I needed some new tyres and so headed to a well known chain of tyre purveyors. Their service was certainly efficient but with the tyres removed and the car 5ft off the ground the specialist informed me that I really needed new brake pads... and discs.... on all four wheels. In fact they were in such bad state they had the potential to severely affect my ability to stop and if left ignored I would surely be killed on the way home. Crikey.

Normally this probably would have spurred me into reaching for the wallet and saying something like "if it has to be done it has to be done". However this time I had insider knowledge. A few months previous to this my car was recalled by the manufacturer due to a fatal fault that had been discovered and had in fact led to the death of several people. The dealer did a complete check up on the car and compiled a detailed report on any potential repairs that may need to be done. They concluded that the tyres would need replaced soon but that everything else was tip top, a small crack was appearing in the exhaust but that was largely insignificant. More importantly the brake discs were in perfect working order. Armed with this knowledge I was able to confidently decline the offer of paying the requested £650 for new ones.

My suspicions were raised further when the other half took her car into the same place for a puncture repair and she was told her brake discs needed replaced too. Luckily she too had the good sense to just say no.

I returned this year for another couple of tyres, brake discs were never mentioned, they must have regenerated themselves since my last visit. Instead this time my track rod ends had seized. £180 to replace them. Based on previous experience I declined and asked my regular mechanic to check them. Strangely he could find nothing wrong with them at all.

This sort of thing is not exclusive to the motor industry, any sort of trade or service can be abused by unscrupulous individuals. Builders, plumbers, financial advisors, dentists opticians and all manner of sales people can convince you that you need whatever they deem to be necessary. They are the expert and you are the idiot standing with an open wallet and nodding your head in agreement with whatever they tell you.

I often wonder how far up the ladder this practise goes. Of course the average trade person can add a bit extra here and there and you will be none the wiser but what if doctors or surgeons did this? "Yes, the bypass operation went well, but while we were in there we noticed your spleen looked a bit dodgy and one kidney was worn so we removed them, better to be safe than sorry!"

I'm going to brush up on my medical knowledge just incase some unscrupulous doctor decides to harvest my organs in some sort of two for one special simply to finance the new brakes on his Jaguar.

Call me cynical but when the crack in my exhaust widens to a point that requires repair I will not be handing over my liver unnecessarily.

A Chicken Walks Into A Hospital…

What does the 5th July 1948 mean to you? Probably not much, but this was a day that had the potential to save your life, even if you hadn't been born yet.

The name Sylvia Beckingham probably means nothing to you either but on the 5th July 1948 she was admitted to a Manchester hospital for treatment on her liver. She was the first person to be treated under the Labour Health minister Nye Bevan's new National Health Service. There are few things that almost everyone can agree was a good idea but the National Health Service must be one of them. Of course it has its problems and inefficiencies but when compared to the health care systems of other countries it shines like a beacon of hope for all who need it. It is truly one of the greatest concepts this country has ever had.

When you are born the NHS delivers you and cares for you free of charge, this continues until the day you die.

I spent quite a bit of time in the hospital as a child. I was born a bit early and wasn't in the best of shape for the first few years but things turned out ok in the end. Without the NHS the outcome might have been very different, at the very least you would be reading someone else's book right now.

As I got older my hospital and doctor visits became less frequent and I slipped into the general pattern most males live by, that is to avoid doctors like the plague.

I can't really explain this phenomenon but it seems to only affect the males of the species. Women seem to go to the doctor at the drop of a hat, men have to be dragged there kicking and screaming. If a man sees a doctor then it is likely he is already dead and nothing more can be done. We prefer to live on a "give it a week and see basis" and that has worked fine for me, up until recently that is.

It started about two years ago. I thought it was just a bit of indigestion from eating too quickly but turns out there was actually something wrong with me.

It was a Saturday night and I had the house to myself. A rare occasion indeed and one that was to be made the most of. Preparations began early. I had assembled most of the supplies I needed, beer, crisps, chips, whiskey and the ingredients for the biggest mouthwateringly good chicken and bacon burger ever made. After a well spent afternoon of doing absolutely nothing I was beginning to feel the first rumbles of hunger so I headed to the kitchen to make my burger.

I dipped the chicken into the beer batter I had prepared earlier and as it turned golden brown I grilled two slices of succulent maple cured bacon and assembled my dressings and condiments. I placed the chicken on the toasted bun, added the bacon, two slices of smoked applewood cheese and topped the whole thing off with lettuce, mayonnaise and tobacco onions. I headed for my favourite chair, cracked open another beer and prepared myself for the culinary delight that I was about to enjoy. As I took my first bite the opening credits to the James Bond classic Dr No began. I was in heaven. A couple of bites in and I began to sense that something wasn't quite right. My burger, moist and succulent as it was, seemed to be struggling to get to my stomach. It felt like a stone in the middle of my chest. I had felt this before and it usually passed after a couple of minutes but this time was different, it didn't go away. I drank some water, no difference, I merely began to fill up like a blocked sink. After 15 minutes or so I tried to make myself sick but it was to no avail. After this my stomach seemed to sense that something was wrong and it decided to try and regurgitate everything I had ever eaten, but all that came out was watery acid and saliva. This happened continuously at 15 minute intervals for the next three hours until the better half came home from work and found me slumped over the kitchen sink, a drooling spluttering mess. Naturally she enquired as to what had led to this debilitating situation and then suggested that I needed to see someone about it. Of course I said I'd give it a bit and see what happens. I had even set the burger back into the oven in the hope of finishing it later.

I spent all night over the sink bringing up all manner of horrible watery bile. The next morning I relented and decided that medical help was indeed needed. Still expelling bile at 15 minute intervals I headed for A&E. It was now 11am, I had been awake for over 24 hours and was feeling rough. Around 12pm I was triaged and sent to Xray and by 1pm the results were in. These proved inconclusive. After another hour or so a bed was found and the doctor injected a series of muscle relaxants to try and allow any blockage that might be there to pass freely. Nothing happened. The next step was to be admitted to theatre. The doctor was optimistic that I could be seen fairly quickly although he knew there were 7 people booked in ahead of me.

There was nothing more to do but wait, with cardboard kidney dish in hand for my ever growing collection of stomach acid and saliva I headed to the waiting room. The only problem was that the waiting room was full. A seat beside the emergency ambulance entrance would have to do. Over the course of the next 4 hours I spoke to several nurses, filled out several forms and had my ob's taken all in the hospital doorway because there were no beds, no rooms or even a broom cupboard available to use. The place was packed, understaffed and under equipped. The nurses and doctors were rushed off their feet and clearly stretched to the limit but despite this they were professional and attentive.

By 8pm that evening it was realised that I had now been awake for 36 hours, 24 of which I hadn't been able to eat or drink anything. A drip was summoned and vital fluids replenished all while sitting in a chair beside the draughty emergency entrance. By 9pm I was on a trolley and heading deep into the bowels of the hospital. Here the hospital was all but deserted. I saw no other patients, it was quiet and the people now looking after me worked calmly and efficiently. The doctor charged with carrying out the procedure explained what he planned to do. Shove a long tube with a camera on the end of it down my throat, into my stomach and hopefully dislodge the stubborn chicken from its resting place.

I was offered anaesthetic but if I took it I would have to stay for a few hours after to ensure I hadn't died. I declined and endured the procedure without the drugs. It was unpleasant. Very unpleasant, but the good doctor found the chicken resting at the entrance to my stomach and shoved it on through. Once the camera was out the relief was instant. Life was good again. Confident Colonel Sanders had been beaten into submission, I was wheeled into the recovery room which again was all but empty and eerily silent, broken only by the withered groan of a man behind a curtain in the next bed. His moans were sorrowful but routinely interrupted with burps and uncontrollable flatulence. A nurse pulled back the curtain to reveal a pale faced man lying motionless in the bed staring at the ceiling. The ghostly figure spoke between the burps and outbursts of arse wind to apologise for his rudeness. The man was obviously broken. I Asked what happened to him. He simply replied "camera, both ends" nothing more needed to be said, what can you say to that?

Anyway just like being at your grannies I was not allowed to leave until I had something to eat and drink. It was the best water and toast I have ever had.

By midnight I was allowed to leave. 40 hours after my big Saturday night in had begun my ordeal was over. I had spent 13 hours in the hospital, it was cramped, hot, understaffed, under equipped, and underfunded. The staff were overworked, underpaid and seemingly under appreciated by many of the impatient patients waiting in A&E.

This is our NHS and as stretched and as inefficient as it is I am grateful for it. I realise now that I have entered the stage of life where hospital and doctor visits will likely become more frequent again. I could grumble and moan about it but since the 5th of July 1948 everyone is guaranteed whatever medical help they need for free, regardless of wealth, income or social standing and thats something we should all appreciate because someday you will need it.

The only thing troubling me is where that camera had been before it was put down my throat.

Whats This "We" Business

A few months ago I heard a casual comment. It was nothing offensive or vulgar, I barely took it under my notice. Perhaps if I had known the full impact this brief remark was going to have on my life I may have paid more attention to it, or at least taken steps to avoid its consequences.

You have probably heard this type of comment before, likely from someone very close to you. They are usually very subtle in their delivery but thats all an integral part of their evil plan.

The words "I think we should redecorate the bedroom" slipped into the middle of a completely unrelated conversation should have set off all sorts of alarm bells. Sadly it didn't.

Fast forward about six months to a quiet Saturday morning. This was the Easter weekend and the first day of a much deserved few days off work. I had big plans or so I thought. I was going to tidy up the garden, wash the car and do some odd jobs around the house that i'd been putting off since last Christmas. As I saw it, all this could be spread over the week, leaving plenty of time for beer and relaxation. Sitting at the kitchen table in my pyjamas just about to enjoy my second cup of coffee, the door bell rang with an ear piercing ferocity.

I trudged to the door and was greeted by the sight of a burley man brandishing a delivery docket, behind him a large lorry was reversing into my drive. With each beep the lorry made as it reversed ever closer, my dream of a relaxing long weekend slipped further and further away from me.

I stood and watched in disbelief as an army of men brought box after box into my garage. Before long I had lost count of the number of boxes but it must have been somewhere in the region of 20 million. I stood there thinking that somewhere a businessman was sitting on a big pile of my money in his now empty warehouse laughing his head off.

I began to read through the list of items on the pink bit of paper I was holding. Tins of paint, wardrobes, chests of drawers, lamps, a dressing table, mirrors, rugs, blinds, a bed, a mattress and a range of assorted crap that made no sense to me whatsoever. Then it hit me like a brick in the face "I think we should redecorate the bedroom."

The words echoed around my head for what seemed like an eternity. Having enjoyed about 20 minutes of my holiday it was clear that that was all I was going to get. Naturally I enquired as to why I hadn't been informed of this pending delivery and subsequent workload, but I was quickly informed that we had discussed the matter months ago and apparently I had agreed to it. Essentially my lack of objection constituted agreement. Somewhat inevitably, the discussion ended with the "you don't listen to anything I say, do you?" statement. I didn't answer, truth be told I'd stopped listening, I was in mourning for my holiday that had been cruelly and prematurely snatched away from me.

Anyway, I spent the next 4 days emptying the room of what I believed to be perfectly functional furniture and lots of useless crap that had gathered up over the last couple of decades. The walls and ceiling were painted in what I thought was the same colour that was already there. I was reliably corrected by woman that it was in fact a completely different shade of magnolia altogether. Could have fooled me. Next came the construction of endless amounts of flat pack furniture which was to be filled with all the crap that was deemed important enough to keep. I argued the point that large amounts of this stuff was utterly useless but this was an argument I was never going to win. So I gave up.

When I was at school the term "we" was plural and was used to denote a group of people. I now know this to be wrong. The term "we" as the wife uses it actually means "you". Woman took on a purely supervisory role for the duration of the project and dropped in occasionally to give orders and to check on compliance issues, much like the German army dropped in on Poland in 1939.

Any time I had that wasn't spent knocking together flat pack rubbish, looking for lost screwdrivers or washing paint out of my eyes was spent ferrying bundles of uncooperative cardboard, wood and plastic to the rubbish tip. I spent so much time there people began to ask if I worked there. By Monday afternoon I was being invited to the pub for afterwork drinks with the rest of the skip keepers. I had become a kind of rubbish guru, a Stig of the dump if you will.

Anyway by Tuesday evening the room was finished, just in time for me to go back to work for a rest on Wednesday morning. It looked good, even if I do say so myself. I got into our new bed that night, exhausted and bereft of energy and although my arms and legs no longer worked as they should, I felt a great sense of pride and accomplishment. It was worth it and anyway it was only a couple of months until the summer holidays, I could relax properly then. Just as my eyes began to close and I started to drift off into a nice relaxing sleep, I was yanked back into consciousness by a voice that whispered "I think we should do up the garden."

I spotted an empty skip at the rubbish tip, I plan to move in next week, call in and say hello if you're passing.

A Stocking Full Of Misery

Is it just me or is Christmas not what it used to be? When I was a kid Christmas was a magical time full of excitement, wonderment and joy. From the start of December the mood of the whole world seemed to change. The dark winter nights that engulfed the world in November were now warmed with the red and green glow of Christmas. The TV started to show warm fluffy christmas films and the famous Coco-Cola advert confirmed that christmas had officially begun. In school, the teacher was unusually happy. The books were put away and the christmas parties started. Learning went on hold for the best part of a month. The dull dreary streets basked in the glow of christmas lights as busy shoppers hurried to buy last minute gifts and goodies. Everyone seemed happier and the world seemed a much better place.

The excitement peeked on the 24th of December. I can still smell the food my mother cooked on Christmas Eve as it wafted into the snug living room where me and my brother sat watching television.   The cold winter weather outside lashed at the windows while a hot roaring fire burned in the fireplace. These were happy times. Then off to bed for arrival of Santa and his presents. Sleep was next to impossible but eventually exhaustion took over and the fight with the sandman was lost.

Christmas morning arrived early and the presents were pilled high, then the food, mountains of it, family arrived too, lots of them. The house was full of aunts, uncles, grandparents and cousins. It was fantastic. The entire week between Christmas and New Years I always felt was strange, a bit of a twilight zone, most shops were closed and the world slowed down as if in mourning for the year now almost gone. By the first week of January the world seemed a much bleaker place, the lights were gone and the teacher was a bastard again. The warm glow of Christmas was replaced with a decidedly blueish tinge and the harsh reality of life took over again. As an eight year old I thought it would be like this forever.

I'm no longer eight years old and the world has changed. Now Christmas starts well before Halloween. The great yawning chasm between these two holidays simply no longer exists. The sight of christmas stuff in the shops no longer fills me with joy but rather a sense of dread and bewilderment. The warm glow of fairy lights no longer warms the cold wintery sky as I battle my way to work in the snow and rain and trudging around crowded shops for presents and turkey is truly terrible. Most of the family who would have spent christmas at ours are no longer with us and the big day is much more sedate than it was in the past.

I look up at the same sky now as I did as a child but the reindeer and fat jolly man in a red suit fail to appear, instead a huge credit card bill looms over the horizon.

I now realise that Christmas is a hassle best avoided. You always spend far more than you can afford, eat far more than you can stomach and panic buy useless crap that people are too polite to shove back in your face. The happy songs of christmas now make you want to poke pencils in your ears and carol singers are worse than the political wannabes begging for votes at your door around election time. It's not only carol singers that are unwelcome, if a fat man tried to let himself into my house on Christmas Eve he would be met with violence rather than milk and cookies and I won't even mention where Rudolf's carrot would end up.

Christmas as an adult is rubbish but I wouldn't have it any other way.

Death the Final Frontier

As the saying goes, there are two things that you can be absolutely sure of in life, death and taxes. As life rattles relentlessly past you and the years roll by and break into pieces of ever fading memories, both of these things become more prevalent in your mind. You can of course cheat taxes, use all sorts of legal loop holes and hide your financial deals in the mirky grey areas off the coast of the Cayman Islands but with death there are no grey areas. When the reaper comes you must obey and quietly follow.

Think back to when you were a child, a man of 40 seemed like a relic and being 60 was completely preposterous. It was nigh on impossible to think of yourself as anything other than maybe a year or two older than you were, except for the childlike notion that someday you would magically wake up as an astronaut or a racing driver or something. This was just natural, no thought was ever given as to how this might be achieved, it was simply a forgone conclusion. As a 8 year old anything was possible.

Life was an everlasting blank canvas stretching out in front of you, the only limitation was your imagination.   As we get older the canvas gradually becomes stained with life's boring necessities. Things like exams, getting a real job, paying bills, buying a house and working every hour God sends to fill the damn thing with all sorts of useless crap you never really needed all start to take over. The best we can hope for is a couple of weeks holiday a year and the health to keep working until you are 187 so you can pay off your mortgage. You pray to God the car doesn't break down, the roof doesn't leak and you can maintain all of your bodily functions for as long as possible with as much dignity as you can muster. All this continues year after year until you reach that fabled finish line called retirement by which time you're too old, knackered and broken to enjoy your few remaining years before the icy hand of death grabs you by the collar and yanks you into oblivion.

Due to reasons beyond your control and decades of poor economic policies by those in power, by the time you reach retirement the canvas that was once crisp, clean and full of promise has been scribbled on, rubbed out, rained on, torn, tattered, burnt and soiled.   It has taken everything that life has thrown at it and survived. You have survived and that is a feat worth celebrating.

Too many people throw in the towel too soon. They spend their few remaining years on earth quietly sitting in their wing backed chairs, falling asleep halfway through page two of Anglers Weekly while patiently waiting for the sweet release of death. Bollocks to that, give two fingers to the reaper, kick him up the arse and tell him to sod off, I'm not done with life yet.

When you're old you can do all the things you couldn't get away with as a fully functioning responsible adult. No longer must you speak with a guarded tongue and hide behind a veil of social niceness. You can tell people exactly what you think of them, you can park where you damn well please and make everyones life around you a complete misery. They will simply excuse this behaviour by assuming you are somewhat senile but will ultimately conclude you are effectively harmless. You can shout obscenities to strangers in the street, tear up the local park doing doughnuts on your mobility scooter and terrorise the young. You could even tell the Queen to eff off if you so desired. Being old is the equivalent of being given the freedom of the borough, don't waste it.

The way I see it you can follow the normal social convention and sit there slowly turning into a man size Werther's Original or you can get out there and cause havoc. Then when you are truly ready, blast through the pearly gates at a hundred miles an hour safe in the knowledge that during your brief time on this earth you have raised hell. I have no intention of growing old gracefully and those that think I should can go to hell. I urge you to do the same.

Microscopic Misery

A few months ago I saw a small end of news story on the TV about a few people feeling unwell in a place called Wuhan. This would not have even made the news here had some of these unfortunate souls not died. Little did anyone know this little news story would soon affect the entire planet and everyone on it.

I watched this story develop and spread from Wuhan throughout China. Videos began to arrive on my phone of empty streets being disinfected. Sights of people in Biochemical Hazmat suits became common and the death toll began to mount, but still it was on the far side of the world in a city that no one had ever heard off. Then It arrived in several surrounding countries. Still the consensus was that this was a widespread virus outbreak of something called Corona Virus but it was largely confined to the east and was not much to be worried about. Much like the Ebola outbreak in Africa, the SARS outbreak in the middle east, the Bird flu, the Swine Flu and all the other diseases that affected other people in other parts of the world.

Italy was next, the death toll reached into the thousands, cases popped up all over the world, France, Spain and then the UK. I don't know why people were shocked, looking back it was like watching an out of control car careering towards you. There seemed to be lots of time to react to this slow motion rerun but still it hit the UK with a sudden jolt.

Why? We are no different from anyone else on the planet, the UK is not immune to disease, plagues or pestilence. A virus isn't going to halt at the White Cliffs of Dover, do a sudden U-turn and head back out to sea in search of something less British. It does not respect borders or political barriers. Unlike humans it does not discriminate, it does not recognise race, religion, creed or gender. To it we are all the same.

Now just 3 months after the nasty little bastard appeared on the far side of the world, many tens of thousands have died and many millions have been infected. Much of the world is locked away, planes are grounded, businesses are closed, public gatherings are banned and only essential services are running. You can even be arrested for being persistently closer than 2 meters to someone. That was a fate usually reserved for perverts and pests. This little virus has not only infected millions of people, it has also infected every single aspect of our daily lives. Until now you only thought Brexit was everywhere, now it seems largely irrelevant but no doubt it will make a comeback soon.

The madness of panic buying has subsided and everyone has settled into the routine of staying at home. A strange calm has fallen over the country, but this is likely to be the calm before the storm if other countries further down the infection line are anything to go by. No one knows, the future is unknown. To use the popular politicians phrase, we are in unprecedented times and sailing in uncharted waters or maybe more realistically, up excrement creek without a paddle.

As I sit in my favourite chair by the window the view is much the same as usual except for one glaringly obvious change. There are no people, there are no cars and there are no little urchins kicking a ball against my garden wall. Without exception the lights are on and everybody is home. This is the new unexpected reality. It would be nice to think that everyone is doing what they are being asked to do in the effort to stop the spread of this virus and the misery it leaves in its wake. Sadly this is not the case. There are those who simply cannot sit on their arse at home and watch TV for a few weeks until it is over. People who have lay idle on their sofas for decades, ignoring all advice to get some exercise and eat healthily have suddenly become seasoned hillwalkers and fully certified outdoors people. These arse bags now want to walk ten miles ten times a day, have picnics in the park and do the exact opposite of what is required of them. Hordes of people took part in mass queuing after heading out to beauty spots and beaches all over the country the day after we had been told to maintain a social distance and to only venture outside if absolutely necessary. The country is full of absolute idiots. Again see previous references regarding a cull.

During two world wars people sacrificed everything. Many were packed up and sent away to far off shores to live in cold muddy trenches only to be shot and blown to bits because they answered the call when their country needed them. Now all we are being asked to do is to sit in your warm comfortable house, drink tea and watch a bit of TV. No one is shooting at you, no one is dropping bombs on your roof and no one is asking you to do anything more than most would do on an average evening anyway.

Previous generations fought for the freedom that we have today. They survived the bombs and the bullets and now this brave generation are the most vulnerable in society. It seems the very least we can do is stay inside so that they might not die on a hospital bed struggling to breath from the microscopic misery that has invaded our shores. The fact is that many vulnerable people will die because you got ill going to the shops to get that absolutely necessary packet of chewing gum. Or because you are simply oblivious to the fact that there is more to the world than what you can see past the end of your own nose.

Speaking of seeing past the end of your own nose, Mr Trump is doing his best to keep the world entertained in these dark times with his daily rants and outbursts of utter stupidity. I would ask you to join me in raising a glass of your favourite high powered cleaning product to salute his unwavering efforts. It would be wrong to single out this particular clown for there seems to be many in the circus. There is a Brazilian that still refuses to acknowledge there is a problem despite thousands of his people dying, his health service on the verge of collapse and large sections of real estate are being turned into mass graves. There is a man from Belarus that says there is no virus because he can't see it and no one around him is currently ill. All manner of weirdos, crackpots and simpletons spouting miracle cures, remedies and ill-advised advice are emerging from the woodwork. Worse still some people believe them.

It's not all bad news, there have been tremendous acts of kindness and compassion all around the world. This reminds us that in general the vast majority of people are good and humanity still has a heart of gold under the tarnished veneer that until recently seemed impenetrable.

I often thought that if there was another world war our country would not stand a chance because of the general selfishness and ambivalence of modern life. Gladly I may be wrong about this. People are looking out for each other, volunteering to deliver food and medicine to those in need. Thousands of medical professionals who had spent their lives working and serving the public and then quite rightly and deservedly retired are coming back into service to do what they can. In just 24 hours over half a million ordinary people answered the government's call and volunteered to help our country in its time of need.

People all across the world have been hanging out of windows and standing on door steps giving a round of applause to the doctors and nurses working around the clock to save lives under extraordinary circumstances and at great personal danger. They know they are probably going to get the virus at some stage but still they work on and sadly some have already succumbed to the disease. Incredible people like Tom Moore, the 100 year old army captain began walking round his house to raise money for the NHS. This hero has raised over £32 million and has become a symbol of hope for the nation. The selfless efforts of this old man walking around his garden to help others puts to shame those who simply can't even sit on their arse and do absolutely nothing in the interests of others.

At this time of great strain and stress people learn to deal with things in different ways. Some will dance, some will sing, some will cry. Some will rediscover faded family ties, conversations will be had and time will be spent together that would not have happened otherwise. Some people will learn new skills and read books that would never have been read. Some will play games and laugh together, others will suffer tragic losses and mourn alone, but when the disease has gone and people slowly emerge into the world again, we can grieve together and hopefully be equipped with a better tolerance and understanding of each other. Hopefully then people will lack the selfishness and narrow mindedness that we have become accustomed to and we will appreciate the world for the wonderful place it is and our neighbours for the wonderful people they are.

Then again people have short memories....

Thank You

I hope you enjoyed reading the inane ramblings of an old(ish) man and you can now go forth and bring newfound grumpiness to the world. I must admit a piece about a worldwide pandemic that extinguished so many lives and affected the entire planet was not how I had expected to finish this book. I was intending to finish with some witty and fatuous comments about life and death but that seems somewhat inappropriate and wrong at the present time.

Since I started writing this book I have been reminded how fragile life is and how easily we all take our way of life for granted. Perhaps now we can see how insignificant we are in this world when a small, invisible little virus can change so much in the blink of an eye.

Our big shinny office blocks which once stood as a testament to human achievement, stand empty and lifeless. Our multilane highways, busy streets and bustling shopping centres are now deserted. Life in the forests, glens and meadows goes on undisturbed, oblivious to the plight that has befallen mankind. The beautiful Italian Lakes, the Grand Canyon and the Great Barrier

Reef are all still there, only the people have gone. Nature and the earth will get on just fine without us.

I have no doubt that life will eventually return to what it was before, but hopefully we will remember that we are not the masters of this universe that we thought we were, but merely guests on this wonderful pale blue dot. I cannot wait to get back out into the world and enjoy all the things I have lamented over in this book. If I am spared, rest assured I will still be grumpy but I will appreciate it all the more.

Good luck to you and remember, don't let the bastards grind you down.

Printed in Great Britain
by Amazon